It was time to make a name for ourselves.

"We're finally sixth graders, Gretch! Top of the heap!" I said.

"But next year, we'll be back down at the bottom again, Kobie. When we go to junior high."

"Don't think about that. Concentrate on making this our most memorable year at Centreville."

"How are we going to make this year memorable?" Gretchen wanted to know.

"We need a new project," I declared. "Something that will make us famous."

Now that we were both almost twelve, it was time to make a name for ourselves.

Other Apple Paperbacks
you will enjoy:

GOING ON TWELVE

Candice F. Ransom

AN
APPLE
PAPERBACK

SCHOLASTIC INC.
New York Toronto London Auckland Sydney

ISBN 0-590-43525-6

12 11 10 9 8 7 6 5 4 3 2 1   9/8 1 2 3/9

For Howard,
who has crossed the equator
for the last time

Chapter 1

"I'll bet anything he's the Hammer Man," I said. Actually, the legend of the Hammer Man had just popped into my mind. But the thought lodged there and grew fizzy, like an m&m dropped in a Coke bottle. Suddenly it seemed more than possible — no, absolutely *right* — that the old man on the hill was really the Hammer Man.

Gretchen took the digging spoon from its place in the dogwood tree. "The Hammer Man? Who's that?"

I parted the heavy veil of honeysuckle to spy on the gray house on the hill above our school. In a mysterious voice, I told Gretchen the story, making up only a little. "Years and years ago, before we were born, the Hammer Man used to sneak around Manassas after dark and hit people over the head with this big hammer he carried hooked in his belt."

1

"Did he kill them?" Gretchen looked up from digging in the floor of our hideout, her blue eyes wide. Usually she didn't mind scary stories, as long as it was broad daylight.

"Well, he didn't do them any good," I replied, quoting my father. Sometimes my parents talked about stuff in the newspaper at supper, forgetting I was there, taking it all in. My father would mention somebody got hit by a car or something and my mother would say, "Isn't it a shame a person couldn't walk down the street?" and then I'd ask if the guy died and my father would answer, "Well, it didn't do him any good."

Gretchen shivered in the dappled light of our Honeysuckle Hideout, even though it was September and still warm. "Kobie, if he's the Hammer Man, how come he's here in Centreville? Manassas is only six miles from here. Why haven't the police caught him yet?"

"Because" — I paused dramatically — "he's very clever. Sure, you'd think a murderer would run as far away as he could. Alaska or someplace. But the Hammer Man was smart. He decided to go where people would least expect to find him. Centreville was perfect. People are so out of it here, even if he went screaming down Braddock Road with his hammer, nobody'd notice."

Gretchen sat back on her heels, the digging spoon loose in her fingers, and stared at the house looming above our hideout. "A real-live murderer right next to our school," she murmured. "Do you think we should report him to the principal?"

I could see us storming into Mr. Magyn's office with the shocking news. Mr. Magyn would react the way he always did, whether a kid came in with a hurt knee or somebody whacked a baseball through the window. Before he'd move from behind his desk, he'd ask Miss Warren, the school secretary, for the proper form. Miss Warren would paw through the filing cabinet, looking under "H" for "Hammer," and then "M" for "Murderer."

I shook my head. "We need evidence first."

"What kind of evidence?"

I let the curtain of honeysuckle fall back. "Hammers," I said. "He probably has a whole rack of them in his basement, maybe with little tags on them so he could remember who — "

The bell rang. Recess was over. It was time to line up on the blacktop.

"Darn. We haven't put our dues in yet.

Gretch, hurry up." Today was Dues Day. We couldn't leave without putting our dues in the tin box.

She scraped dirt off the lid of our buried box with her bare hands and pried it open. I threw in the nickel I had been saving. Gretchen tossed in a quarter. She always had more money than I did. Then we piled the dirt back in the hole and stamped on the earth so no one would realize anything had been buried there. Not that anybody had discovered our secret hideout yet.

Because Gretchen was the tallest, she wedged the digging spoon in a V-shaped branch of the dogwood tree. Then we scrambled out of the tunnel, yanked the honeysuckle vines over the secret entrance, and scurried up the hill to join the rest of our class.

We got in line behind Vincent Wheatly, the meanest boy in the whole school, let alone the sixth grade, and giggled. We had done it again! Mrs. Harmon never missed us — we had spent the entire recess period in our hideout instead of playing dumb old four-square.

"Class!" Mrs. Harmon blew her whistle so hard I expected to see smoke fly out of her ears. "Next week we begin physical fitness training. Boys and girls are to bring shorts and T-shirts for that week. I'll pass out the permission slips at the end of the day."

I groaned. The President's program for fitness was the pits. Last year, in fifth grade, our teacher forced us to jump and throw and catch like trained seals. We performed dashes and sit-ups and the most loathsome event of all, the six hundred. Now, I don't mind running ten or even fifty yards, but eight times around the blacktop is ridiculous. I walked the course, pulling the worst time in the history of Centreville Elementary, thirteen minutes and twenty-three seconds. And I didn't even get out of breath.

"It's not so bad." Gretchen tugged her strawberry-blond ponytail over one shoulder. "We'll probably be partners again like we were last year."

"I'm going to get a doctor's note," I said, knowing full well my mother would eagerly sign the permission slip. She was forever driving me out of the shade where I liked to sit and read, into the hot, broiling sun and urging me to play like a normal kid. "Maybe I'll break my leg before next week," I said hopefully.

Mrs. Harmon herded us back inside. In room 10, I sat down and scratched "Kobie Roberts" in the soft wood of my desktop with the end of my pen. I'd been working on my name-carving since the first day of school. Mrs. Harmon caught me in the act the second day and gave me a lecture about defacing school property and how I'd have to pay for my desk. But then I showed her the fifteen other signatures carved on the seat and the back of the desk and she clammed up.

In the desk beside me, Gretchen took out her history book. She was always ready to start the lesson, even before the teacher told us to take out our books. She looked over and saw me inking the "K" in my carving.

"Kobie, you shouldn't write on your desk."

"Why not? Everybody else does." I indicated the signatures I wasn't sitting on. "I want all those nerdy little kids coming after us to know I was here. We're finally sixth graders, Gretch! Top of the heap!"

She thoughtfully chewed the end of her pencil. "That's true. After five years, we're number one. But next year, we'll be back down at the bottom again, Kobie. When we go to junior high."

"Don't think about that. Concentrate on making this our most memorable year at Centreville. When we leave, I want people to say, 'The old place will never be the same without Kobie Roberts and Gretchen Farris.' "

"Well, they'll have the 'old' part right, anyway," Gretchen laughed.

That was another reason I didn't sweat over carving my name in my desk. All the furniture and equipment were practically falling apart. Centreville Elementary was one of the oldest schools in Fairfax County, Virginia. My father went here when he was a little boy, so our school was either forty or a hundred and eight years old, I forget which. My father worked for the grounds department of Fairfax County schools and he was always telling me about the nice new schools the kids in Annandale and Burke went to. Next year Gretchen and I might go to one of those new schools.

"How are we going to make this year memorable?" Gretchen wanted to know. Mrs. Harmon was late getting the history lesson started. She was busy yelling at Vincent Wheatly for cutting a chunk out of Marcia Dittier's hair. With Marcia's looks, one hank of hair wasn't any great loss.

Instead of answering Gretchen, I stared out the window to the playground below. Just beyond the edge of the blacktop, I could see our hideout, last year's secret project. One day at recess, we discovered that the honeysuckle-tangled dogwoods bordering the school property would make a terrific hiding place. We sneaked away from the rest of the class every day during recess to tunnel out weeds and vines. We also got terrible poison ivy but it was worth it. When we were finished, our hideout had a packed-earth floor and a thick canopy of vines that let us see out but kept outsiders from looking in.

I brought an old spoon from home and Gretchen found an old tin box which we buried in the dirt floor. Every other Thursday was Dues Day. We added to the treasury whatever we could afford. At the end of the year, we planned to buy the Nancy Drew books we didn't have.

If I craned my neck a little, I could spot the old man's house on the hill above the Honeysuckle Hideout. At least, an old man was *supposed* to live there, but no one ever saw him. I didn't even know his name.

The biggest problem with dinky places like Centreville and Willow Springs, where I lived, was that nothing ever happened. *Nothing.* In the mystery books Gretchen and I checked out of the library, kids were always having adventures, tracking down jewel thieves or finding long-lost treasures. All we ever did was get up, go to school, do homework, and go to bed. In between, our parents made us clean our rooms and sometimes we visited relatives in Mannassas, the next town over. That was it.

"We need a new project," I declared. "Something that will make us famous."

"Like what?" Gretchen asked.

"Like — " My eyes went to the gray house on the hill again. "Like finding out the truth about that old hermit next door. That he really was — is — the Hammer Man."

"Gosh, Kobie, I don't know. . . ." Gretchen's voice trailed off. She turned to the end-of-the-chapter questions in her history book, already leery of my project. Okay, so one or two of my schemes hadn't worked out. That was no reason to reject the best idea ever.

I wasn't too worried about Gretchen. We'd been best friends since second grade. No matter what I wanted to do, she'd go along. Now that we were both almost twelve, it was time for us to make a name for ourselves. And revealing the true identity of the Hammer Man would do it.

I jumped off the bus, feeling weightless and free the way I always did at the end of the school day. Setting my books on a flat rock, I opened the mailbox and pulled out two bills and an ad. I noticed my father's hand-painted "Roberts" was coming off again. He'd painted our name on the mailbox so many times I could see faint outlines of the old letters peering around the new ones like jiggly ghosts.

Gretchen and I both lived in Willow Springs, a place so dinky it didn't qualify as a town. Gretchen lived a few miles down Lee Highway. We rode the same bus, but I got off first. After supper, she'd call me and we'd do our homework together over the phone.

I headed up our long, steep driveway. In the summer, briar roses and morning glories spilled down the bank next to the garden. Now the garden was weedy, September-neglected. A few dead-ripe tomatoes, hidden among the weeds, the skins wrinkled and split, reminded me of forgotten Easter eggs. Summer was definitely over.

At the crest of our driveway, I planted one foot firmly on a fist-sized white rock I called the Moonstone. It was embedded in the gravel and polished smooth by the tires of our car. Every single day, whether I was going up the driveway or down, I stepped on the rock because I believed it brought me luck. Today I skipped back to tromp on the Moonstone a second time, for good measure. If Gretchen and I were going to expose a desperate criminal like the Hammer Man, we needed all the luck we could get.

In the kitchen, I found my mother ironing a plain white dress. Another white cotton dress, freshly-pressed, hung from the doorway. On the windowsill, a cooling apple pie scented the air with cinnamon. It was nice to be home.

"Did you make me those little pie dough things?" I asked, heaving my books onto a chair.

"Don't I always?" my mother replied. "Over there on the stove."

I poured myself a glass of cherry Kool-Aid, totally unsweetened the way I like it, and took the pie plate and my glass over to the table Whenever my mother made a pie, she rolled the dough scraps in cinnamon and sugar and baked them for me. To me, the scraps tasted better than the pie.

"How was school?" My mother adjusted a sleeve before pressing it.

"Boring, as usual." Of course, I couldn't tell her about the Honeysuckle Hideout or the new project Gretchen and I had dreamed up just today. My mother believed kids should be thrilled to go to school and learn long division. If I told her I had fun, she'd automatically assume I was carrying on and not listening to the teacher.

I ate the last pie dough roll-up and stared at the white dress as she slipped it on a hanger. "That looks like a uniform."

"It is. I've got a job."

"A job! Where? You can't even drive!"

She unfolded a stack of aprons and began pressing them. "I don't need to drive to this job. I can take the bus."

"When did you get a job?" I couldn't believe it. My mother was always home, like the shabby old sofa in the living room. It would be funny not to see her when I came home from school.

"Today." She bent over the ironing board, concentrating on a wrinkle. "I was up at your school and you didn't even know it."

"You were at my school? Why?"

"To get a *job*, silly. I work in the cafeteria now — well, starting Monday."

I nearly splashed the apron with cherry Kool-Aid. "You're going to be a cafeteria lady? In *my* school?" My voice shrilled like Mrs. Harmon's when she was trying to get Vincent Wheatly to behave. "How could you *do* this to me?"

She stopped ironing. "Do what? Kobie, we need the money. Taxes this year are sky-high . . . and I'd like to buy new living room furniture. So I decided to get a job. I wish you wouldn't stare at me like that. It's not the end of the world."

"Yes it is!" I shrieked. "Mom, you *can't* work in my school! It's — against the law! There's some law that says a parent can't go to the same school as her kid!"

"There is not. Mrs Wright teaches sixth grade and her two girls go to Centreville. Maryruth is in your class instead of her mother's and it's no problem."

Not unless you considered the fact that Maryruth Wright was a 'fraidy-cat wimp scared of her own shadow. And who wouldn't be? Maryruth could hardly misbehave or talk back to the teacher, not with her own mother in the very next classroom. Now *my* mother was going to be downstairs in the cafeteria This was worse than the time in fourth grade when she volunteered to be room mother. Whenever we had a party, my mother would sail in with her box of cookies and party hats and stay until it was time to go home. Needless to say, I never had much fun.

Instead of bringing cookies to my class four or five times a year — a punishment I'd gladly endure — now my mother would hand me my plate in the lunch line *every single day*. She'd watch me eating and giggling with Gretchen. She'd see me blowing straw wrappers. She'd know when I traded my entire lunch for somebody's dessert. I'd never be out of her sight. The image was too horrible to bear.

"Why did you get a job as a cafeteria lady?" I wailed. "Why didn't you try the fountain at Centreville Pharmacy if you wanted to cook so bad?"

"Kobie, I wasn't really looking for a cooking job," she explained. "I wanted a job that would let me be here when you got home from school. Working in your school seemed the best solution. And of course, there's the bus."

A nasty feeling squirmed in the pit of my stomach. "What bus?" I asked warily.

"Your bus. I can take the school bus to and from work every day. I won't have to beg rides. It works out perfectly."

"You mean, you're going to ride my *bus*, too? Stand out at *my* bus stop and wait for the bus with *me*?" This was getting worse by the minute. "Mom, you can't do that! The school bus is just for kids. The only grown-up allowed is Mr. Bass, the bus driver."

"I don't know where you get these strange ideas. I've already talked to Mr. Bass and he said he'd be delighted to have me ride his bus." She frowned. "But you aren't. What's bothering you?"

I was too overwhelmed by her news to reply. My mother working in the cafeteria, riding my bus . . . I wouldn't have one speck of privacy, anywhere!

"Kobie, this job is a good thing. We'll have more money — your father won't have to work so much overtime. He'll be able to build you that tree house you've been wanting."

I perked up a little at that. Ever since my father saw me attempting to build a tree house with one board and four nails, he promised to build me a real tree house, with walls and a roof and everything. But summer had come and gone and still no tree house. My father had worked every Saturday and spent the evenings in the garden.

"Do you think Dad will start my tree house this weekend?" I asked, tears springing to my eyes. Even if my father built me a tree house city, it wouldn't help the fact that my wonderful sixth grade year was over before it began. Gretchen and I might as well kiss our secret project good-bye. No way could we trap the Hammer Man with my mother hovering around.

She came over and gave me a squeeze.

"It's tough being an only child, isn't it? We try to make time for you, Kobie, but it isn't always possible, with all the bills we have."

If she hadn't acted nice, I would have been okay. If we had gone on arguing about her stupid job at my school, I wouldn't have started crying like a baby. I hated to cry — I was going on *twelve*, for Pete's sake.

I broke away from her, blubbering like a first grader. "I don't care what you do!" I yelled. "But don't expect me to sit by you on the bus! And I'm fixing my own lunch from now on — I'd rather die than eat your dumb old food!"

Chapter 2

When I called Gretchen and told her about my mother's new job, she didn't seem to think it was the end of the world, either.

"Your mother can give you double helpings of French fries," she said. "And sneak you extra butter cookies." The great big round butter cookies the cafeteria served, usually on Flying Saucer Sandwich days, were worth buying lunch for.

"I'll get double helpings, all right," I said bitterly. "A double dose of problems. Gretch, can you just *imagine* having your mother work in the cafeteria of your school? Can't you just hear my mother nagging me to eat all my lima beans in front of everybody?"

"Kobie, it probably won't be so bad. Don't worry yourself sick over it." Papers rustled on her end of the line. "I hate to change the subject, but have you done your arithmetic?"

"I looked at it. You know I can't do long division. Will you give me your answers?" I wheedled.

"Yeah, but Mrs. Harmon wants to see how you got them."

"I know." In the drawer of the phone stand, I scrounged up a pencil stub and an old envelope. "Maybe I can figure it out backward once I have the answers."

"Kobie, long division is easy. Wait till we get to fractions and decimals." Gretchen always peeked ahead in her textbooks to see what was coming up next. As for me, I always hoped that after the chapter we were working on, my book would be filled with blank pages.

"Why did you have to bring that up? I'll never be able to do fractions or decimals or long division. I can't even do short division."

She sighed. "Kobie, short division is like multiplication, only in reverse, kind of."

I didn't want to talk about arithmetic. Gretchen could explain it to me until she was blue in the face, but I only knew my times tables up to five and that was why I couldn't divide. The rest of the times tables — six, seven, eight and especially nine — were too slippery to stay in my brain.

"This was supposed to be such a great school year," I grumbled. "First we have that awful physical fitness training. Then we have long division. Now my mother will be spying on me in the cafeteria and riding my bus! What else will go wrong?"

"Nothing," Gretchen replied confidently. "Bad things come in threes. Only good things can happen from now on."

After we hung up, I went down to the basement. Usually I watched TV or talked to my mother while she cooked supper, but today I wanted to be by myself.

I sat on the steps, breathing in the cool, musty air. The basement was one of my favorite places. Both sides of the white plaster stairwell were covered with my drawings. Once a long time ago when I was bored and didn't have any paper, I started drawing in the stairwell. Naturally my mother complained, but my father told her my drawings were cheaper than wallpaper.

I didn't feel very creative, so I went over to my swing. When my old, rusty swing set had to be hauled to the dump, my father salvaged one of the swings, looping the chains over a big, square metal beam in the basement. I rocked back and forth, glad nobody from school could see me. The chains grated overhead, *skreek! skreek!*

Next to the swing was a mildewed carton

of ancient encyclopedias. The encyclopedia we used at school was divided alphabetically — "Timbuktu to Wombat," for example. But each volume of my old encyclopedia was a separate subject, like *Science, Peoples of the World*, etc. The books had rich-looking dark blue bindings, and were filled with old-fashioned pictures. The information in them was mostly out of date. Once my teacher asked me how many planets were in the solar system and I told her seven. "My encyclopedia says so," I argued when she informed me I was wrong.

I loved to idle in my swing and leaf through those books. It made me feel content. I picked up the Children's volume, which had the neatest pictures, and opened it on my lap.

But all I could think about was my mother in her white uniform standing at the bus stop with me Monday morning. The bus would come and we'd get on together. She'd make me sit with her, in the seat right behind the driver where the goody-goodies sat.

The encyclopedia grew heavy in my lap. The cellar seemed gloomy and damp, no longer pleasantly cool. Suddenly I knew what my name would be this year, the name everyone would remember me by: Mama's Baby.

On Monday morning, I stood as far away from my mother as I possibly could and still legally be in our driveway. We waited for the bus without speaking to each other. She was mad at me for acting so childish over a little thing like her riding my bus. Little thing!

When the bus came, I charged on first, butting in front of my mother to save a seat for Gretchen. My mother took forever getting up the steps and then she had to stop and talk to Mr. Bass, the bus driver. It was so embarrassing. Mr. Bass wasn't allowed to start the bus again until everybody was sitting down. Traffic backed up behind us something terrible.

My mother looked around uncertainly. She glanced over where I was stubbornly claiming the middle of an empty seat, then glanced away. A little red-haired girl piped up, "You can sit with me!" My mother slid next to the little girl, smoothing her uniform over her knees. We did not look at each other.

When Gretchen got on, she said hi to my mother and would have said more but I pulled her away.

"Don't encourage her. Maybe she'll leave us alone."

"But she's not bothering us," Gretchen pointed out.

"She will."

At the unloading zone at school, my mother poked down the steps in her thick-soled white shoes.

"Your mother is very nice," Mr. Bass said as I stomped off the bus. "I'm glad she'll be riding with us."

"Well, *I'm* not." It was beginning already. Pretty soon everybody would be associating me with my mother. I was doomed.

The little kid my mother had sat with on the bus was having trouble with the front door. She smiled at me as I opened it for her. "Is that lady your mother?" she asked.

"What's it to you?" I asked sourly.

In room 10, I threw the paper sack containing the shorts and T-shirt I had to wear during recess in the cloakroom, stuffed my lunch bag under my desk, and flopped in my seat. I was too depressed to work on my name-carving.

It was an awful day, just as I expected. First, we had to switch arithmetic homework to mark in class. When I handed mine to Gretchen, Mrs. Harmon plucked it out of her fingers and gave it to Kathy Stall on the other side of the aisle.

"You girls are too chummy," Mrs. Harmon declared. "I want you to start mixing with your classmates more, Kobie."

As the teacher called out the answers to the arithmetic questions, I saw Kathy cheerfully checking every one of mine wrong, because I hadn't written out the whole problem. Kathy, of course, got them all correct. I wrote a very small, very faint "A" in the corner under Kathy's name.

"You failed," Kathy said loudly as we switched papers back. "You missed them all," she added unnecessarily. The "F" she had scrawled at the top of my paper was as big as the Empire State Building.

And Mrs. Harmon wanted me to "mix" with the other kids. Everybody in my class, in the whole school even, except Gretchen, was a total nerd. I mean, with friends like Kathy Stall, who needed enemies? Mrs. Harmon didn't understand that Gretchen and I were more than friends — we were practically sisters. We liked exactly the same things, mystery stories and butter cookies and talking about how we were going to be famous when we grew up. The other girls were dull as sticks — all they ever wanted to do was play jumprope. The reason Gretchen and I made the Honeysuckle Hideout was to get away from them.

Recess made the morning seem like a picnic. We changed into shorts and T-shirts in the girls' room and met the boys on the blacktop. Vincent Wheatly whistled at Kathy Stall, who looked nice in shorts. In fact, all the girls but me looked good in shorts. I had the skinniest legs in both sixth grade classes. Nobody whistled at me.

The first event was the broad jump. We were supposed to jump across this sawdust-filled pit as far as we could. Mrs. Harmon marked everyone's jump with a yardstick. She didn't need a yardstick to measure mine — a six-inch ruler was more than adequate. When I lumbered to my feet, brushing sawdust off my shorts, I was mortified to see my footprints were barely over the starting line. My broad jump was more like a bunny hop.

"Let's hear it for Bony Maroni! Hey, Skinny Minnie!" Richard Supinger yelled. He was Vincent Wheatly's sidekick.

I wanted to run down the hill to the Honeysuckle Hideout, but Mrs. Harmon's whistle urged us on to the next event.

"Don't pay any attention to them," Gretchen said. "They're just stupid boys."

"Gretchen, I can't broad jump and I

can't do long division. I'm a sixth grade failure. Washed up at eleven!"

After we had sprinted and hopped and choked ourselves at the chin-up bars, Mrs. Harmon decided we had been tortured enough for one day and let us go early. As I changed into my dress, I realized I still had lunch, with my mother as a cafeteria lady, to look forward to.

But when we got back to class, two things happened to make me forget about my mother, for a little while, at least.

We had a new kid. He shuffled shyly beside Mrs. Harmon's desk, staring at the floor while she introduced him.

"Class, I want you to welcome John Orrin to room 10," she said. "His family moved to Centreville last week. Let's show John how glad we are to have him join us."

I applauded with two fingers, smirking at Gretchen.

John Orrin was a shrimp, even smaller than me. He had hay-colored hair and watery gray eyes. When he walked back to the desk Mrs. Harmon assigned him, two seats over from me, he ducked his head and loped like a camel.

Gretchen and I cracked up behind our geography books. He was so funny-looking! He reminded me of a scarecrow, with that straw hair and those too-short pants. On the back of my "F" arithmetic paper I sketched a scarecrow. Scribbling the caption "John Oreo" at the bottom, I passed the drawing to Gretchen. She spluttered with laughter.

Mrs. Harmon was down the aisle like a shot. "What's going on here?"

"N-nothing," Gretchen stammered. She tried to slide my sketch under her geography book, but the teacher snatched it from her.

Mrs. Harmon stuffed the drawing in her pocket, flashing her glasses in my direction. "Kobie, see me before lunch."

The whole class was staring at me, including the new boy. My face burning, I pretended to read a terribly interesting paragraph in my geography book. When I looked up again, only the new boy was still watching me. He was actually smiling, as if he thought it was hilarious that I was in trouble with the teacher. I stuck my tongue out at him and he turned away.

Then Mrs. Harmon made her second announcement.

"Settle down, people. As you know, our annual Back-to-School Night is October 15. Every year, all the classes do special projects for the parents to see. This year, the two sixth grade rooms will compete to display their project on the bulletin board by the office." Immediately a buzz of excitement swelled and Mrs. Harmon had to flick the lights on and off to get everybody quiet again. "Mrs. Wright and I have already selected the subject and type of project. We are going to do a mural sewn on burlap. A medieval tapestry showing a scene from the Middle Ages we're learning about in history."

Right away there were a million comments, mostly from the boys, who didn't like the idea of sewing. I wasn't crazy about the sewing part myself, but I knew somebody had to draw the picture on the burlap and I wanted to be that person.

"Everyone will participate in the project," Mrs. Harmon said, bringing a chorus of groans from the boys. "We will all help design the mural and each of you will take a turn stitching the design — "

I couldn't stand it any longer. "Who's going to draw the picture?" I blurted out.

"Did I see your hand raised, Kobie?"

I waggled my fingers and waited for her to call on me. "Who's going to be the one who draws the picture?"

"Why, everyone," Mrs. Harmon replied.

"Won't the design look better if *one* person draws it?" I said. "If a whole bunch of people work on it, it'll look like something from Miss Dede's room." Miss Dede taught first grade. A few kids snickered.

Gretchen held up her hand. "Mrs. Harmon, I think the best artist in the class should draw the design." Surprisingly, Kathy Stall and Marcia Dittier and a couple others agreed with her.

"I don't know," Mrs. Harmon hesitated. "It hardly seems fair to let one person do the entire drawing. . . ."

"But we want to win!" Vincent Wheatly bellowed. "We want to beat Mrs. Wright's class!"

"Yeah!"

Mrs. Harmon relented. "We'll take a vote. All those in favor of one person drawing the mural, raise your hand."

I raised both of mine. The majority ruled; it was decided that one person would draw the tapestry.

"How are we going to determine who the artist should be? Suggestions?" Mrs. Harmon perched on top of her desk.

That was easy. The best artist was seven seats away from her. But I couldn't nominate myself. I elbowed Gretchen.

"Mrs. Harmon," Gretchen spoke up. "Kobie Roberts is the best artist in our class. Last year, Kobie and Lynette

O'Bannon were picked to do the theater show."

The fifth grade in room 8 did a theater show every year. Two artists illustrated a fairy tale on a long paper scroll. Then the scroll was stretched on dowels in a fancy little wooden theater and rolled like a film-strip. Last year, Lynette and I drew "Cinderella." We copied the pictures from a Golden Book, working during free periods. Then we wheeled the portable theater around to all the lower grades. Lynette turned the scroll while I read the story to the little kids.

"Lynette will probably draw the mural for Mrs. Wright's class," Kathy Stall said. Lynette O'Bannon was in room 11, the other sixth grade class.

"If we want to win, we ought to let Skinnie Minnie — I mean, Kobie draw ours," Richard Supinger said, grinning at me.

"Richard, do you want to spend lunch in Mr. Magyn's office?" Mrs. Harmon said sternly. "All right, let's take another vote. Those who want Kobie Roberts to draw the design for our mural, raise your hands."

It was unanimous! I was elected to draw the tapestry. But, then, I *was* the best artist in the class.

On my way to lunch, Mrs. Harmon snared me. Gretchen waited at the door, but the teacher motioned her on. When everyone had left, Mrs. Harmon took the scarecrow drawing of John Orrin from her pocket. She laid it on her desk between us.

"One thing I won't tolerate in my class is cruel humor," she began. "You didn't have to write John's name below your drawing — you *are* a good artist. Your caricature is quite accurate."

"What's a cari — what you just said?" I asked.

"A picture of a person with their features exaggerated and distorted. I suppose you think this is very funny."

"Well, yes. Don't you? You said yourself it looks just like him — "

"Kobie, don't get smart with me. You are deliberately misreading my point. What if John Orrin had seen this picture? How do you think he would have felt?"

But he *hadn't* seen the drawing, I almost protested. Why worry over something that hadn't even happened? However, I suspected my best-artist title was at stake. "It probably would've hurt his feelings," I said humbly.

"Exactly. Now would you have wanted to

hurt his feelings? A brand-new student, his first day here?"

I shook my head. Mrs. Harmon tore the drawing to shreds and dropped the pieces in her trash can.

"Can I go to lunch now?"

"You may. But remember, Kobie — the other students voted you best artist in the class, a great honor, but I will take that privilege away from you any time I see you abusing it. Do you understand?"

I nodded that I did. Then I grabbed my lunch bag and skipped down the stairs to the lunchroom. Maybe I couldn't do long division or broad jumps, but I was the best artist in my class. Soon I'd be Best Artist in Centreville Elementary, when our mural won the contest. Now *that* was a name people would remember.

Chapter 3

The rackety engine of my father's old Ford tractor coughed twice, then died. My father clambered down from the seat and came over to sit by me on the big flat rock at the edge of the garden.

"Just look at that sky," he said, tipping his cap back. "Not a cloud in it. October is my favorite month."

"Mine, too." I hugged my notebook to my chest. Every year when October rolled around, cool and serene after a muggy September, we made the same statement.

"Great month to work outdoors," my father went on. "Not too hot. No birds twittering."

We both listened. Though woods surrounded our property, we didn't hear a single bird.

I liked having the same favorite month

as my father. "I wish my birthday was in October. On Halloween. That'd be neat."

"I wish my birthday was in October, too." He stretched out his legs. The cuffs of his dark green pants were caked with red clay. "But we had to be born in July, didn't we? I guess that makes us appreciate October even more."

In the fall my father plowed the garden one last time before winter, turning over the tasseled weeds and dried-up cornstalks until the earth was red and clean again. Usually I rode on the tractor with him, snugly wedged between his shoulder and the chipped fender. I'd watch the action behind us, hoping the plow blades would bring a white quartz arrowhead or a battered Confederate bullet to the surface.

But today I was too busy to help plow. Since I was going on twelve, I figured riding the tractor was for kids, and anyway, I hardly ever found an arrowhead or a musket ball.

I sat on the flat rock at the edge of the garden and worked on the mural sketches. Our class had finally decided on a scene for our medieval tapestry — a medieval castle, a dragon running from some knights on horseback, and a unicorn grazing in a flowery meadow. Yesterday Mrs. Harmon excused me from social studies so I could go to the library and check out books on the Middle Ages.

"What are you doing?" my father asked. "Every time I look, you've got a pencil in your hand."

I showed him my picture of the castle. "It's for our Back-to-School Night project."

He held the tablet out at arm's length, studying my drawing. "That's really something, Kobie, the way you can draw. I couldn't draw a straight line with a ruler. I can't even draw flies."

I giggled because he always said that. "I'm having trouble with these horses." On the next page were sketches of stump-legged horses. "I can't get their legs right."

"They look fine to me." He tilted his head. "Did you hear that one snort?"

"Oh, Dad." I swatted him with my drawing tablet.

"Well, with the garden all plowed, I've got a little free time next weekend," he said. "Have you thought about where you want your tree house?"

My heart leaped. He was actually going to build my tree house! I pointed to an oak on the other side of the driveway. "Over there."

"Kobie, that tree doesn't have any low branches to hold a tree house. The trunk goes straight up for twenty feet. It won't work."

I flipped to the last page in my drawing tablet. "It'll work if you make it like this." In science class last year, I had designed a tree house that didn't need to be built around large, sturdy branches. Instead, the structure was fastened to the *side* of the tree, with braces underneath.

"Yes, that'll work," he acknowledged. "I would never have thought of building it tacked to the tree like that."

"I got the idea from a book about these kids trying to build a clubhouse, only they don't have a tree big enough so they just build a house on stilts." Now for the sticky part. "Can you make me stairs like this, Dad, with rails on both sides?"

"You don't want a ladder? Most tree houses have rungs nailed to the trunk of the tree."

I shook my head. As desperately as I wanted a tree house — a secret place all my own, away from my mother — I was afraid of heights. Once I got *up* there, I knew I'd be okay, but I couldn't stand to climb ladders. I hardly ever went into our attic because the pull-down stairs were so narrow they scared me.

"I can build a staircase, if that's what you want."

"And don't make it very high," I said. Then I added hastily, afraid he'd change his mind if I made too many demands, "I mean, you won't have to build such a *long* staircase if the tree house is kind of close to the ground."

"A close-to-the-ground tree house. Sounds more like a bush house to me." He chuckled. "Tell you the truth, I don't like high places, either. When I was in the Navy, they put me in the crow's nest once for a four-hour watch. The crow's nest was way above the deck and every time the ocean pitched, that pole dipped so low I thought I'd have to bail water."

"How did you get down?" For me, getting down from a high place was almost as bad as climbing up.

"I skinned over the fella coming up to relieve my watch. Practically ripped his shirt off him."

I loved to hear my father talk about his Navy days in the Pacific. He had been to Australia and a lot of islands with magical-sounding names like Guam, Borneo, and New Guinea. One island had nothing on it but pure white sand like sugar and big dumb birds that couldn't fly. No people, no animals, not even any trees. It sounded so different from dreary Willow Springs.

"Tell me about the time you crossed the equator," I asked.

"Oh, you've heard that old one a hundred times. You don't want to hear it again."

"Yes, I do! Please, Dad!"

When he laughed, I knew he intended to tell me all along. He was always teasing me. "When I was in basic training up in Great Lakes, Illinois, some of the guys told awful tales about crossing the equator. Seamen who'd never been that far south before had to pass an initiation ceremony."

"Like eating cold spaghetti blindfolded and they tell you it's worms?" One year at the school Halloween party, the older kids did that to the younger kids.

"I wish it had been cold spaghetti. Well, the day arrived. Our ship was about to cross the equator. All of us who were going to be initiated were blindfolded and lined up on deck. Some guy slammed me in a barber chair and the ship's barber shaved me bald. Then he flicked a lever under the chair and threw me backward over the railing. The whole way down I thought I'd been thrown overboard! I landed in a big tub of seawater on the lower deck, only I didn't know it. I thrashed around like a whale, trying to get that blindfold off and get to the top! When I climbed out, everybody was laughing. But I was one of them — I had crossed."

With my pen I aided a sluggish ladybug on her descent from the rock to the grass. "Did you feel any different?"

"I was wet — and plenty mad."

"No, I mean, when your ship was right at the equator. Did you feel funny being on the line?"

"Kobie, the equator isn't actually a line, like you draw on paper. It's an imaginary circle around the earth that divides the Northern Hemisphere from the Southern Hemisphere. You can't really see it."

"But you must have seen *something*," I insisted.

"No, I didn't. Those are just numbers, Kobie, coordinates the captain uses to guide the ship. The equator marks the base line for latitude. Have you learned about latitude and longitude in geography yet?"

I shook my head, more interested in what it felt like to be right on the equator, not really in the Northern Hemisphere and not really in the Southern Hemisphere. Now that I was going on twelve, I seemed to be drifting toward some kind of equator myself. I wouldn't be a real teenager until I was thirteen, my mother had told me, and I was phasing out being a kid. In July, I'd turn twelve . . . and be right on the line. I wanted to know what I was in for.

My father thought I was still stuck on latitude and longitude. "I've got a paper somewhere," he said. "When I passed the initiation."

"What kind of paper?" I'd never heard this part of the story before.

"A certificate signed by King Neptune. Everybody got one when we crossed. It had the latitude and longitude and some other stuff about the mysteries of the deep, or some such craziness."

A paper signed by King Neptune, about crossing a mysterious line! If I had that paper, I'd really *know*. "Where is it, Dad? Do you still have it?"

He shrugged. "Your mother has all my military papers. She'll get it for you."

My heart sank. Ever since my mother had begun working at my school, she had less time for me than she usually did. On weekends, she was busy cleaning the house and doing laundry.

"No, she won't," I said.

"All you have to do is ask her."

I could ask *him* to do things for me, like build my tree house and tell me stories, but my mother wasn't at all like my father.

* * *

Our special table in the lunchroom was conveniently located near the garbage cans and away from the monitors. To discourage anyone else from sitting with us, I propped the extra chairs against the edge of the table, like the janitor did when he mopped the floor. It was the only way Gretchen and I could have complete privacy.

While Gretchen was inching through the lunch line, I dumped out the contents of my lunch bag. A few minutes later, she sat down with her tray.

"Here's your milk," she said, handing me the extra carton off her tray. "Your mother wants to know when you're going to stop acting silly and come through the line to buy your own milk."

I unwrapped the sandwich I had slapped together that morning — Vienna sausage, sliced lengthwise and lined up on the bread. "Fingers again."

Gretchen stopped buttering her roll to give me a dark look. "Kobie, why do you always have to be gross at lunch?"

"That's the only time it counts." I laughed, but I was really angry with my mother, passing that message to Gretchen. The serving line was so noisy, I knew my mother had to yell it out. Probably every kid in school heard her tell Gretchen how silly I was behaving.

"Your mom also said to eat all of your lunch," Gretchen reported. "She knows you threw your banana away yesterday."

"That banana was rotten," I said. "She made me take it, even after I told her I didn't want it. You see how she is? My mother has spies everywhere in here but under the table — I have to bring my lunch to save my reputation."

I finished half my sandwich, but put the other half on Gretchen's tray to throw away without my mother noticing. Today I had slathered too much mayonnaise on my sandwich. I was tired of Vienna sausage anyway, and that made me even madder because normally I loved it. Another favorite thing down the tubes since my mother started working at my school.

"Look who's coming," Gretchen whispered suddenly.

John Orrin was ambling in our direction, clutching his tray and scanning the room for an empty seat. His head swiveled like a lighthouse beam. John was last in the lunch line every single day, not just because he hadn't made any friends who would let him cut in front, but because he was so slow. A snail crawling over molasses moved faster than he did.

"He's on free lunch," I said. Actually it

was no big secret. Everybody knew he was on free lunch because Mrs. Settinger, the cafeteria lady who collected the lunch money, screamed, "Go on through!" to the kids who didn't have to pay.

"So what?" Gretchen said. "Lots of kids can't afford to buy lunch."

"I know," I replied quickly. My mother was forever reminding me how poor *we* were, yet we always had enough to eat. Whenever I went through the serving line behind a kid on the free lunch program, I always felt a little peculiar. Lunch was just lunch to me, but according to my mother, lunch to those kids was often the only meal they got all day.

Today I didn't care whether John was a welfare case or not; I didn't want our meeting interrupted. "He can't sit here." I jerked the extra chairs around us, barricading our table from the intruder.

"I think he's going to. The monitor probably sent him over here."

"Rats. I wanted to talk about the old man next door."

"We'll talk about it some other time," Gretchen said, as John approached.

I didn't want to be put off. Too many portions of my life were out of my control now. "Go away," I told John as he gingerly set his tray down.

"Kobie!" Gretchen looked shocked.

"The lady told me to sit here," John drawled. He had a weird accent, real hicky.

"She didn't ask *us* if you could sit here." I glared at him. "This is a private table. Members only."

Gretchen shoved one of the extra chairs toward John. "Kobie was just fooling. Sit down. Your food will get cold."

"Who cares?" I muttered, but John sat down anyway, undaunted by my glare.

Gretchen kicked me under the table. "Kobie, what's the matter with you?" she hissed.

I kicked her back, hard. "What's the matter with *you*? Why don't you roll out the red carpet for him? Buy him a box of Oreos? You got a crush on him or what?"

She bit her bottom lip. Her shin must have hurt from my kick, but she didn't cry.

"I don't think I want to be friends with you anymore," she said softly.

I flung my trash in the garbage can. "Fine! I don't want to be friends with you, either."

Down the table, John Orrin dug into his lunch. Apparently terminal slowness did not affect his appetite. He smiled at us placidly around a mouthful of mexi-corn, either secretly glad or completely unaware of the tension he'd caused between me and Gretchen.

For the rest of the day, Gretchen and I avoided each other, which wasn't easy considering our desks were side by side. We didn't play hangman or giggle like we usually did. It was a long afternoon and I was glad when the last bell rang.

I followed Gretchen on the bus. She paused before our special seat, third from the front on the left. Then she saw me and stepped back to let me pass.

"Go ahead," I told her.

"No, you go in."

"You were here first."

Gretchen took the seat, sliding over close to the window. "Aren't you going to sit here?"

"Are you sure you want me to?" I was blocking the aisle but dynamite couldn't have moved me. Gretchen and I hardly ever fought. I was desperate to make up with her.

"Are you sure *you* want to?" she countered.

I sat down beside her. "I'm sorry — "

"I'm sorry — " she began at the same instant.

Automatically we chorused "Thumbs up" and held up our right thumbs in the required signal. We kept on chanting

"Thumbs up! Thumbs up!" at the same time, until Gretchen collapsed with laughter.

"We have to link pinkies," I instructed. We crooked our pinky fingers together to end the jinx of talking at the same time. "I hate it when we fight."

"Me, too. I didn't mean it when I said I didn't want to be friends with you anymore."

"Neither did I. I've been miserable all day," I confessed. Never again, I vowed, would I fight with Gretchen over something as stupid as John Orrin sitting at our lunch table. It wasn't worth it.

"There's your mother," Gretchen said. "She looks tired."

My mother *did* look tired as she plodded down the aisle, but it was her own fault. Nobody forced her to get a job at my school.

"Who's that girl who saves your mother a seat every day?"

"I don't know." I pretended not to notice my mother and the first grader, one seat ahead of us. "Some dumb kid. Her name's Beverly."

"She really seems to like your mother."

Beverly and my mother were going to town up there, chattering like they hadn't seen each other in years.

"My mother loves little kids who don't

have any front teeth," I remarked sarcastically.

Now Beverly pulled a wad of paper from her Barbie lunch box. The paper was a big, oatmeal-colored sheet of construction paper, the cheap kind issued to the lower grades. On it Beverly had crayoned a lopsided house and a messy-looking thing that could have been either a person or an elephant with measles — it was impossible to tell.

"Isn't that cute?" Gretchen cooed.

"What a crummy picture! I could draw better with my feet!" An unfamiliar emotion churned in my stomach, like the time I had too much grape soda at the fireman's carnival and then got on the Round-Up ride.

My mother exclaimed over Beverly's picture, praising it enthusiastically.

"Your mother thinks it's cute," Gretchen observed.

"She doesn't know *anything* about art," I said. "She doesn't know anything about anything. I wish she'd never got that dumb job. All she does is bug me."

"How can you say that? She's not bothering us one bit. You don't want your mother sitting with us and she isn't. What's eating you?"

What was eating me was the sight of

Beverly's gap-toothed grin as she hugged my mother's arm. Gretchen was half right — I didn't want my mother sitting with us. But I didn't want anybody *else* sitting with her, either.

Chapter 4

"One of us could go up and knock on his front door and ask him directions or something. You know, distract him, while the other peeps in his windows." I kept my voice low since we were in the library at school. "Then, when we find which room has the evidence we need, we go back and try to get it."

Gretchen frowned. "And just how do we get in his house? Walk up and say, 'Pardon me, but my friend wants to borrow one of your hammers. We're going to take it to the police and have you arrested.' Kobie, if the Hammer Man's been hiding out here all these years, he's not about to let two kids go off with one of his hammers."

"Of course we're not going to *ask* him for a hammer," I said, forgetting to keep my voice down. "What kind of a jerk do you think I am?"

"Just an ordinary, everyday one." Gretchen grinned, unable to resist making the crack.

"Very funny." I surveyed the library over the book I was holding in front of us to help muffle our conversation. Another class was filing in to join ours. "We have to come up with a foolproof plan. This is a desperate criminal we're dealing with, Gretchen."

"How do you know that? I mean, why does the old man on the hill have to be the Hammer Man? Suppose he's just some old man who doesn't like to leave his house?"

"Honestly, Gretch, you're getting as fussy as Harmon. Why *can't* he be the Hammer Man?" Mrs. Sharp, the librarian, warned me with a nod. I lowered my voice again. "The Hammer Man disappeared without a trace years ago, right after his last murder. The police never found a single clue and you know why? Because he's right here, that's why."

Gretchen turned the pages of a horse book until she found a picture I could copy. "Here's a good one. He's running like the horse in your mural. I still don't see what makes you think he's the Hammer Man."

I began sketching the running horse in my notebook. I had finished the castle and the meadow parts of the mural. The horses, and the unicorn, which was basically a white horse with a horn, were driving me nuts. I couldn't get their legs right to save me.

"That's just it," I said briskly. "I *think* he's the Hammer Man. You have to think of something first, before you find it out. That's how electricity got invented. Benjamin Franklin thought it up first — he probably got tired of drippy candles — and then he went out with his kite and got struck by lightning."

Since she needed further convincing, I elaborated on my theory. "Take Nancy Drew. She doesn't sit around waiting for criminals to fall in her lap. She *deduces* who they are, by using her mind. I've already deduced he's the Hammer Man — all we have to do is think of a plan to catch him."

Capturing a murderer would make me instantly famous. I'd be the Centreville Heroine. Of course, having the name Best Artist in Centreville Elementary wouldn't be so bad, either. I could handle both.

"One more thing, Sherlock," Gretchen said.

I concentrated on the horse's legs, trying to get the proportions accurate. "What's that?"

"How are we going to catch the Hammer

Man when we're not allowed off school property?"

I looked up from my sketch to stare at her. Sometimes Gretchen was so sensible, it was annoying. "We sneak off school property, that's how."

"But, Kobie, it's against the rules. Mr. Magyn could suspend us. My mother would kill me if I got suspended."

I wasn't surprised Gretchen was worried about a minor detail like leaving school property. She never turned in homework papers full of eraser holes. And she never yelled in class or threw spitballs. At the beginning of the year when Mrs. Harmon told us to put covers on our schoolbooks to keep them nice, Gretchen spent one entire evening converting grocery bags into book covers. She wasn't exactly a teacher's pet or anything like that, but she never caused any trouble, either. The most daring thing Gretchen did was skip recess with me to meet in the Honeysuckle Hideout.

"Gretchen, if we get caught, it'll be for a good reason. It won't be like we're running off to the Dairy Queen."

The ice-cream stand, Centreville's no-man's-land, was located at the bottom of the hill opposite the old man's front yard, like an oasis in a desert. Occasionally a kid would get a craving for frozen custard and slip away during lunch. The principal forbade the students on pain of death to walk over to the Dairy Queen during school hours. We even thought twice about going to the Dairy Queen *after* school.

I could see this was a big thing with Gretchen. Our project was in danger of disintegrating before it ever got off the ground unless I did something.

The other class, Mr. Breg's fifth grade, swarmed over the bookshelves. Two classes at once packed the tiny library. Mrs. Sharp came over to our table.

"I haven't had a chance to speak to you girls this morning," she said. "Kobie, I see you're still drawing."

"She's working on the mural for our room." Gretchen told her about the sixth grade competition.

"Is there anything I can do for you? Any books you need?" Mrs. Sharp was the neatest person in the whole school. She had long dark hair she wore pulled back and sparkling black eyes. She was never too busy and always had interesting articles and books in her office she saved just for Gretchen and me. Library period was very special because of her.

"Do you have anything about wringing a confession from a criminal?" I asked seriously.

Mrs. Sharp laughed. "Oh, dear, I'm afraid we're fresh out of books on that subject. What are you two up to now? Last year you kept hounding me for books on buried treasure."

"Oh, we're still interested in treasure books," I put in quickly, with a sidelong glance at Gretchen. You couldn't always trust grown-ups, even the nicest ones. If Mrs. Sharp knew what we were really up to, she'd probably feel obligated to go to Mr. Magyn and blab. "Do you have any new ones?"

"Not at the moment, Kobie, but I did come across an article in *Life* about a lost mine somewhere out west. It's just the kind of thing you'd like. I don't have the magazine with me, but I'll bring it in next week." The other class was getting rowdy. Before she went over to calm them down, she wished me good luck on the mural.

"She's really nice," Gretchen said. "I like her a lot."

"Me, too," I replied absently. I was staring at a straw-haired girl in Mr. Breg's class. "Is that John Orrin's sister? Another one? Boy, those Orrin kids are everywhere."

Orrins overran Centreville Elementary like field mice in a granary. They were easy to spot since they all had the same haystack hair and pale gray eyes. There was an Orrin boy or girl in every grade and two Orrins in the sixth grade, one in each class. John's older sister Brenda, who was at least fourteen and had obviously flunked out, was in Mrs. Wright's class.

"Maryruth told me they ride her bus," Gretchen said. "She said when the Orrins get on, there's no room for anybody else."

"They ought to have a bus of their own," I commented. "Where do they live?"

"On that dirt road off Union Mill. Maryruth says it's sort of a shack. It must be awful to be that poor."

I didn't want to think about how poor John Orrin's family was. It wasn't my fault his family didn't have enough money. Library period was almost over. We still had to figure out a way to trap the Hammer Man. But first, I had to get Gretchen over her silly fear of leaving school property.

When Mrs. Harmon announced it was time to begin social studies, I stood up, stretched importantly, then strolled over to the long row of cabinets where the art supplies were stored.

I was excused from social studies every day until I finished drawing the mural. Yesterday Mrs. Harmon asked how much longer I would be and I told her artists shouldn't be rushed. After all, Michelangelo had lain on his back for years painting the ceiling of the Sistine Chapel and nobody bugged him to hurry up, it was almost Back-to-School Night.

While the others labored over boring old social studies, I took out my box of colored chalk and prepared to hoist myself up on the cabinet. Mrs. Harmon had tacked the length of burlap that was going to be our tapestry mural over the supply cabinets, the only available wall space. In order to transfer my drawings in chalk onto the burlap, I had to climb up on the cabinet and sit cross-legged on the countertop. After a while in this position, my legs cramped and I realized how much in common I had with Michelangelo.

The cabinet was too high for a short person like me — not so high I was scared to climb up, but high enough to make me look ridiculous getting up there. Today I was chalking in the outlines of the knights and horses, which meant I would be working practically in the sink.

I put my hands on the edge of the cupboard, hoping to spring up in one smooth, coordinated move. But the toe of my shoe bumped the stupid cabinet knob and threw me off balance. Scrambling to gain a foothold on the slick wood, I dove headfirst into the sink. Fortunately it was not filled with water, but my cool move was certainly demolished.

With my tennis shoes braced against the faucet, I began sketching with a piece of dark blue chalk. The rest of the class had their heads bent over their textbooks, reading. Everybody except John Orrin. He was staring at me, with a sliver of a smile. I knew he had seen my giraffe-leap up on the cupboard and thought it was funny. For some reason, his little smile irked me so bad I smudged the horse I was outlining.

Recess followed social studies. Physical fitness training was over. I had scored the lowest in both sixth grades in every event, but I didn't care. Sports were dumb.

For the first time in over two weeks, I led the way into the Honeysuckle Hideout.

"Boy, I thought we'd never get back here," I said to Gretchen, closing the screen of vines that concealed the secret entrance.

"It has been a while." Gretchen agreed as she checked to make sure the digging spoon was still in the dogwood tree. "Everything's just like we left it."

I parted the vines so I could see the games in progress on the blacktop. "I wonder why nobody has discovered this place yet. We've been coming here almost two years."

"Maybe it's because only the swings and merry-go-round are down here. The boys usually play in the softball field and the girls are always up on the blacktop. Only little kids come down here to play."

"I guess that's it." The dodgeball game certainly didn't fascinate me. I moved to the other side of the hideout so I could spy on the Hammer Man's house. "I bet he's up in that house, probably going through his scrapbook of all his favorite unsolved murder cases. Murders that he committed — "

"Kobie, don't start that," Gretchen said, nervously finger-combing her ponytail.

"Okay." I could tell she wasn't in the mood for spooky stories. Maybe because it was October and there was a strangeness in the air, a deadly quiet. The house on the hill was creepy, occupied, yet you never saw a living soul around the place. Still, I had to get her over being scared to leave school property. And then I spotted the perfect excuse.

"What's that?" I said suddenly.

Gretchen looked in the direction I was pointing. "What's what?"

"That. Over there in the vines. Looks like an old fence." The area beyond the hideout, on the old man's property, was carpeted with brambles and more honeysuckle. A rusty-black bar arrowed up through the weeds. "Let's go see."

"I don't know. . . ." Gretchen glanced back over her shoulder to see if Mrs. Harmon was watching us.

"Gretch, don't worry about Harmon," I told her. "We're only going two steps from the hideout. The bushes will be in the way. She'll never see us."

Actually it was more like ten yards from our hideout to the fence section. The weeds were so thick it took us ages to get there. Beggar's-lice clung to our socks.

"Here's your old fence," Gretchen said. "That's all it is. Now let's go back."

I tried to lift the fence, but it was too heavy. "People don't put up fences just for the fun of it. This was here for a reason, either to keep people out of something . . . or to keep something in."

"It's just a fence, Kobie. Come on." From here we were in plain view of the old man's house. Gretchen kept flinging uneasy glances up the hill.

I felt a little funny myself. The old man could be watching us from his window. It was time to go back anyhow. I was about to tell Gretchen that she had left school property and nothing drastic had happened to her when I tripped over a rock and went sprawling. The rock, half-buried under a snarl of vines, was square and solid.

"Now I know why this fence is here," I cried. "This is a cemetery! I've found a gravestone!"

Gretchen blanched. The idea of a cemetery on the property of a possible murderer obviously gave her the willies. "Kobie, let's get out of here. Right now!"

I was tearing honeysuckle away from the tombstone. "Darn. It's just a rock, after all. It's only shaped like a gravestone."

"Good. Now we can leave." She yanked impatiently at my jacket.

"No, wait. Gretch, here's another rock. And another one. I wonder why somebody put these rocks here. They go in a circle, see? Help me." I uncovered five square stones from a jungle of honeysuckle. The rocks had been set in a circular pattern, and were webbed with vines. Nobody had been down here in years.

Reluctantly she helped me clear the weeds from the last rock. The last weeds came away in one big bunch, revealing a deep hole beneath the vines. My arms plunged into nothingness. I skittered away from the rock-rimmed edge, my heart pounding. To me, a deep hole in the ground was just as frightening as climbing a ladder.

"It's a well," Gretchen noted. "An old dried-up well. I guess somebody had it fenced off at one time. Do you think we should tell Mrs. Harmon about it?"

Recovered from my fright, I headed toward the Honeysuckle Hideout again. When we were inside I answered her. "She won't care. It's not on school property."

Gretchen flared with anger. "Kobie Roberts, you did this on purpose! You couldn't rest until you got me to leave school property, could you? Suppose Mrs. Harmon saw us?"

"But she *didn't*. Gretch, you've got to stop being so afraid of teachers. Mrs. Harmon doesn't run the world."

"Neither do you, Kobie!" She was madder that I had ever seen her, even madder than the day I wouldn't let John Orrin sit at our table.

"Gretch, I did it for your own good."

She never lost her temper with me, not even the time I pleaded with her to give me all her book-fair money to buy an Advent calendar simply because I liked the sparkly village scene and the little doors to open each day before Christmas. But now she was furious. "You didn't do it for my own good. You did it to see if your plan would work. Just because you come up with the best ideas doesn't mean I'm going to follow you and get in all kinds of trouble. Ever since we've been friends, you've always told me what to do and I'm tired of — "

"Shhhhhh!" I clamped my hand over Gretchen's mouth. "Somebody's out there. They probably heard you yelling."

We stood stock-still in the center of our hideout. As long as no one discovered the secret entrance, we were safe.

"Who is it?" Gretchen whispered.

I twitched aside a blackberry vine to see better. The person lurking outside our hideout stooped as he peered into the bushes. I drew back, more shocked than upset.

"It's John Orrin," I breathed. "What's *he* doing here?"

Chapter 5

I had forgotten about my father's King Neptune paper until I was cleaning some old drawings out from under my bed one Saturday and suddenly remembered it. My mother would know where it was. The sooner I found that paper, the sooner I'd know what I'd be in for after I turned twelve.

My mother was baking cupcakes to put in the freezer. She was also making a big pan of lasagna to freeze for supper one night when she didn't feel like cooking.

"Cook, cook, cook," she said as I walked in the kitchen. "That's all I ever do. Some days I get so sick of it, I wish I could — "

"Could what? Quit your job?" I supplied for her, hoping she'd take me up on the offer.

"I can't do that," she said, vigorously stirring the frosting. "We need the money."

I gazed longingly at the frosting bowl. As usual, my mother had made only enough icing to barely cover the cupcakes, so I had no chance of licking the bowl. "I hope that's not your usual flour-and-water icing. That stuff hardens like plaster of paris."

"I do *not* make frosting out of flour and water," she retorted. "I'll have you know I use powdered sugar and milk and real butter."

"Then how come it gets so hard? I almost broke my teeth last week." Now that I took my lunch instead of buying, I begged her to buy lots of goodies like Twinkies and those little bags of Fritos. But my mother claimed that five packs of Twinkies every week was too expensive so she baked cupcakes and put them in the freezer for my lunches. "Gretchen's mother makes the fluffiest frosting. Her cakes are yummy."

My mother paused to give me her you're-skating-on-thin-ice look. I got that look from her a lot lately. I decided to drop the cupcake issue while I was still ahead.

"Dad said you had his Neptune paper. Would you get it for me?"

"What? A Neptune paper? What on earth are you talking about?"

I hooked my finger in the frosting bowl while she was busy knocking cupcakes out of the muffin tins. "It's this paper he got in the Navy when he crossed the equator, signed by King Neptune. He says it's with his military papers and that you know where they are. He told me I could have his Neptune paper."

"I don't know anything about any Neptune paper." She put a teaspoon of icing on a cupcake. "I have his discharge paper from the Navy and that's it."

"But you have to have the Neptune paper," I cried. "He said you do. Look for it, please!"

"Kobie, I've got a hundred things to do this morning without stopping to dig through a bunch of papers. I have to finish these cupcakes and that lasagna . . . iron my uniform and polish my white shoes. I don't have time for your foolishness."

"You never have time for anything I want to do," I accused, swiping a big hunk of frosting. She caught me this time and cracked my knuckles with the frosting spoon. "All you ever do is work."

"Do you think I love serving all those ungrateful kids who come through my line and gripe?" she said. "When you get older, you'll have to work, too. Either at home or at a job or both."

Being a grown-up sounded like a real drag to me, endless worrying about taxes and fuel oil and new tires for the car. In a way, I felt sorry for my mother. But in a way I didn't. After all, she had gone to my school and got that job in the cafeteria on her own — nobody made her do it. Then it occurred to me that she really hated her job and didn't know how to get out of it.

"Listen," I told her conspiratorially. "All you have to do is not wash your uniform or polish your shoes. Mrs. Settinger will see you're messy and she'll fire you. That's what I did when I wanted to get out of bus patrols."

Last year in fifth grade, the captain of the patrols selected me to replace a patrol who couldn't keep up his "B" average. At first I was thrilled to be a patrol. I got to wear a white canvas belt with a silver badge. Every Monday morning, I was excused from the pledge of allegiance to go to a patrols' meeting and I was allowed to leave class early at the end of the day. I felt really cool when I marched out on the highway with my red flag to halt the cars.

But after a while, I hated going to those meetings and I never had any fun on the bus because I had to sit up front with Mr. Bass and hold the flag. It was like being in the Army. I decided to get myself kicked out by not washing my patrol belt. We were supposed to wash our belts over the weekend so the patrol captain could inspect them on Monday. My patrol belt got grubbier and grubbier and when the captain asked me if I had washed my belt I kept telling him I forgot. The kid I was replacing raised his grade average and the captain kicked me off patrols. I gladly turned in my badge and belt.

My mother smiled at my suggestion. "I'm afraid that won't work in my case, Kobie. Anyway, I don't want to get fired. Some days aren't so bad." She finished icing the cupcakes and began wrapping them in waxed paper, leaving two on the plate.

"Can I have those?" I asked, caving in with hunger. It had been a whole hour since breakfast and then all I'd had was four measly slices of French toast and some sausage.

"You may have one cupcake. I'm saving the other."

"For me to have later?"

She ran water in the pan and bowl. "No. It's for somebody else."

"Who? Dad?"

"If you must know, I'm going to give it to Beverly, the little girl I sit with on the bus."

Cupcake crumbs flew out of my mouth as I sputtered indignantly. "*Bev*-erly! You're giving *my* cupcake to that little twerp?"

"It's not *your* cupcake. And she's not a little twerp."

"She is a little twerp. I've seen the way she acts when you get on the bus."

"What's wrong with the way she acts? She's a sweet child."

"She's dumb."

"She is not dumb. You're talking like a child, Kobie. Beverly's six years younger than you are. How do you think you acted when you were her age?"

"I didn't act like that. And I could draw better."

"Yes," my mother agreed. "You're a real artist. But your disposition leaves a great deal to be desired."

"There's nothing wrong with my disposition!" I argued. "It's that little kid, hanging all over you all the time, showing you her pictures and now you're bringing her cupcakes. Next thing, you'll adopt her!"

She laughed at that. "Why, Kobie Roberts, I believe you're jealous!"

"I am not!" I denied hotly. "Why should I be jealous of some little twerp who can't draw and hasn't got any front teeth?"

"Stop calling her that name, Kobie, I'm warning you." Then she put her hand on my forehead, brushing my bangs aside. "What's the matter with my little girl today? Have you got growing pains?"

"My legs don't hurt." Whenever I used to run a lot, my legs would sometimes ache and she'd tell me I had growing pains. I'd measure myself against the sewing room door to see if I had grown any, but I'd always be the same height.

"Your legs don't have to hurt to have growing pains," my mother explained. "You seem out of sorts lately."

I *was* out of sorts and with good reason. Gretchen and I still hadn't come up with a plan to approach the Hammer Man. Report cards would be out in a few weeks and I knew I was flunking arithmetic. And I was really bothered by that new kid, John Orrin. After two years of keeping the Honeysuckle Hideout a secret, some stupid new kid finds it right away. Gretchen and I stayed quiet until he left, but I think he knew we were in there.

My mother slid the lasagna dish in the oven. "Okay," she said, wiping her hands on a tea towel. "I'll go look for that Neptune paper you're pitching a fit over."

In her room, she lifted the green strongbox down from the closet shelf and set it on the bed to unlock it. I hung eagerly over her shoulder. There were loads of documents in the box, insurance policies and birth certificates and contracts. At the very bottom was my father's Navy discharge paper, with a photograph of his ship, the U.S.S. *Griffin*, in the center. But no King Neptune paper.

"It's not in here." My mother began cramming the insurance folders back in the box. "I told you I've never seen such a paper."

"But Dad says he has it." I *had* to have that paper.

"If he does, I don't know where it is. You'll have to ask him again."

"It could be in his drawer," I said, hopping off the bed. My father stored personal belongings in the top drawer of his bureau.

In a flash, my mother collared me. "You know better than to go nosing in your father's things without his permission. You're getting a little too big for your britches these days, young lady."

I jerked away from her. "Well, you were the one who said I was growing up! What do you expect?" I ran before she could scold me for talking back.

But as I dashed out the back door, I heard her call after me, "My mother always told me girls started carrying on when they hit twelve. She didn't miss it by much!"

It felt good to be outside in the fresh autumn air. I barely remembered my grandmother, my mother's mother, because she died years ago. Evidently all she did was run around spouting mottoes for my mother to pass on to me. Stuff like, "Were you brought up in a barn?" when I forgot to shut the door and the one I detested the most, "Life is what you make of it." How could I possibly make anything of my life with my mother breathing down my neck?

Yet her parting remark shook me. According to my grandmother's dire predictions, I was supposed to start carrying on when I hit twelve! I probably wouldn't be able to help it, either. The second I turned twelve, I'd lose control. This was the important stuff I wanted to know. My mother wasn't a very reliable source. I still needed the Neptune paper.

I went out to the shed to ask my father if he knew where the paper was. I found him piling lumber on the wheelbarrow.

"What's that for?"

"Your tree house. Grab my carpenter's apron, will you?" He rolled the wheelbarrow out of the shed.

"You're going to start my tree house right now?" I snatched up his carpenter's apron and hurried after him.

"You bet."

The ladder and the rest of the lumber were already heaped around the base of the tree I had chosen. I watched my father saw the braces that would hold up the tree house and then build the platform. It was tough, slow work, but we talked and that made the time pass faster.

"What's your mother doing?" he asked once.

I looked up from the design I was making with his nails, lining them up by size. "Nothing much. She's so grouchy, I can't stand to be in the same room with her."

"Grouchy, huh?" He planed a board, then said, "Are you sure it's not the other way around?"

"I'm not grouchy! I don't know what her problem is these days, but she just won't get off my case. I can't ever seem to do anything right anymore." I rearranged the nails into a sunburst pattern.

"I know why you can't get along with your mother," he said. "It's because the two of you are exactly alike."

"Mom and me alike? You've got to be kidding. She's *years* older than I am. And we don't look at all alike . . . she's bigger than I am and her eyes are dark brown and her hair's getting gray — "

"I don't mean those things," he interrupted. "I'm talking about the way you both act in general."

I still couldn't see his point. "I don't act like my mother. She's *boring*."

"I guess the things she does seem boring

to you, but believe me, it's easy to tell you're her daughter."

"If we're so much alike, then how come we fight so much? Gretchen and I like the same things, and we hardly ever fight."

"Taking after somebody isn't necessarily the same as liking the same things," he said. "When you get older, you'll understand what I mean."

I hated it when my parents wormed out of telling me the truth by saying I'd understand when I got older. By the time I was old enough to understand all the stuff I'd been trying to figure out since the day I was born, I'd be too old to do anything about it. But never in a million years could my mother be the slightest bit like me. We had absolutely nothing in common.

We stopped for lunch, then went back to work. By three o'clock the platform was fastened to the side of the tree. My father climbed up on the platform to construct the walls, while I stayed on the ground.

"Kobie, don't you want to come up here? You can help me with the roof after I get these walls done."

I shook my head, squinting up at him. "I'll just stay down here."

There was only one way up to the platform, up that skinny, wobbly ladder. Until he built my staircase, I had no hope of getting up to my tree house.

My father leaned out the doorway and looked down at me. "How about if I come down and help you up the ladder? I'll be right behind you every step of the way. I won't let you fall."

I would have given anything to be up where he was, but my feet seemed rooted, earthbound. "I can't," I said, ready to cry. "I just can't."

"Okay. Nobody's going to force you to do anything you don't want to." He ducked back inside and reappeared at one of the long windows, resting his level on the ledge. "Kobie, are you sure you're going to be able to get up the staircase when I build it? This tree house is pretty high. I'd hate to see you too scared to come up here."

That horrible thought had entered my mind, too. What if I couldn't use the staircase, either? What if my father built me this fabulous tree house and it just sat there vacant because I was such a sissy? If the kids at school found out I was too cowardly to climb up to my own tree house, I'd have another name besides Mama's Baby: Kobie the Chicken.

Chapter 6

It sounds pretty dumb to throw away the Best-Artist-in-the-Whole-School title over a cloud, but that's exactly what I did.

On Monday, Mrs. Harmon questioned my progress on the mural. "You're taking too long, Kobie," she said. "Why don't I let some of the others start stitching the castle? We need to get moving on this. Back-to-School Night is a week from today."

Mrs. Harmon might have known about fractions and decimals, but she didn't know beans about art — or the way true artists work.

"I can't finish the background with a bunch of people in the way," I told her. "Just give me one more good day. I could probably finish if I missed arithmetic," I added coyly.

"No, you couldn't, either. You can stay in library period and use that time."

So I remained behind in room 10 while the rest of the class trooped off to the library. The background part of the mural, which I had saved to outline last, was taking forever. Every tree, each flower and blade of grass had to be drawn just so, or the whole effect of the tapestry would be destroyed.

I was working on the sky when the class came back, carrying library books.

Mrs. Harmon came over to check on me. "Kobie, we're going to start stitching after lunch, whether you're done or not."

I resisted the temptation to stick my tongue out at her tweed-covered back. Sometimes Mrs. Harmon was just too pushy, even on projects that were supposed to be fun. She ordered Kathy Stall and Marcia Dittier to untangle and sort the big bag of colored yarns she had brought in. The girls dumped the yarns on the floor right below where I was drawing. I tried to ignore them.

"What is *that*?" Kathy Stall asked suddenly.

I turned around slowly. "What's what?"

"That! That thing you're drawing. What is it?" Kathy pointed to the cloud I had just finished outlining in purple chalk.

Some people are so stupid it's unbelievable. "It's a cloud, dummy. What do you think it is?"

"Looks more like a turtle to me."

"A turtle that was run over by a car!" Marcia commented and they fell over giggling.

Immediately Mrs. Harmon was on the scene. "What's the trouble over here? Marcia? I gave you girls something to do and I expect you to do it *quietly*." Her voice boomed across the room. The entire class was staring at us.

"It's Kobie's cloud," Kathy giggled. "It looks so funny."

Mrs. Harmon stared at my purple cloud. "That's a cloud?"

"Of course!" What was the matter with her? How did she get to be a teacher if she didn't know a cloud when she saw one?

"It looks rather — well. . . ." She pressed her lips together, at a loss to describe my cloud.

"Like a turtle that was run over by a car!" Marcia Dittier repeated, still trying for a cheap laugh.

Mrs. Harmon silenced Marcia with a scowl. "Kobie, that cloud doesn't go with the rest of the mural."

"But, Mrs. Harmon, this is the way you

draw clouds! I learned how from Frank Forrester."

"Who?"

"The weatherman on channel four."

Marcia and Kathy went off into peals of giggles again. "Kobie learned to draw from the weatherman!" Kathy shrieked.

I glared down at them. There was no point explaining to those turkeys — or to my teacher, for that matter — how I spent years lying on my stomach in front of the television while my father watched the news, waiting for Frank Forrester to come on. The weatherman could draw so cool, he just grabbed a Magic Marker and made fast, practiced motions and there was a sun hidden by a fog or big splashy raindrops. His clouds were the best — flat on the bottom, swoopy-scalloped on the top, the way clouds really *are*, most of the time. My version of Frank Forrester's cloud was particularly good.

But you couldn't expect peasants to understand anything about art. "Mrs. Harmon," I said tightly. "This is the right way to draw a cloud."

"But it doesn't *look* like a cloud," she maintained. "It spoils the rest of the mural."

"It does!" Kathy said, sticking her two

cents' worth in. "I think we ought to let somebody else draw the clouds."

. I nudged her head with my foot. "Who asked you?"

"Kobie, stop it," Mrs. Harmon commanded. "You shouldn't be so sensitive. After all, other people are entitled to have opinions."

"Not if they're stupid!"

"That's enough, Kobie." Then she said, "It's really too much work for one person, this whole mural. You're probably tired. We'll see what the others think. All those in favor of keeping Kobie's cloud, raise your hands."

Two hands waved in the air, mine and Gretchen's. John Orrin had his arm half lifted, as if he couldn't make up his mind whether he liked my cloud or not. But he didn't count. Why weren't Vincent Wheatly and Richard Supinger supporting me? They were the most influential boys in room 10 — if they voted yes, everyone else would, too. But their hands stayed stubbornly down.

I wanted to punch out Kathy Stall and Marcia Dittier. It was all *their* fault this whole mess got started. They had been so eager to have me draw the mural in the first place and now they were criticizing my cloud. That was another reason I never mingled with those girls: they were two-faced.

"We'll get someone to help Kobie with the background," Mrs. Harmon declared. "It's better this way, Kobie." She smiled to cushion the blow. "With two of you working, we'll be able to begin stitching this afternoon. You've worked very hard on the mural and you've done a wonderful job. Won't it be nice to have someone help you finish?"

"No, it won't!" But I didn't say it very loud.

Mrs. Harmon scouted the class for a suitable helper. Kids whose arms were apparently made of lead a few minutes before now waved wildly, dying to be picked. My only hope was that she would choose Gretchen. A hope that was quickly dashed.

"How about . . . John! John Orrin. You've been very quiet." Sure he was quiet — nobody ever talked to him. "Come up here, John. Kobie will show you what to do."

I would? Of all the people she had to pick! The *one* kid who got under my skin, and now he was going to work on my mural.

"Mrs. Harmon," I said brusquely. "I've changed my mind about putting clouds in the mural. We really don't need them. A bunch of clouds only makes the picture too fussy — "

"Don't be silly, Kobie. Of course we're going to have clouds." She handed John another piece of purple chalk. "Start by redrawing Kobie's cloud."

He had even more trouble than I did climbing up on the cabinet. With a sheepish glance at me, he rubbed out my beautiful Frank Forrester cloud with the heel of his hand and awkwardly drew a plump, marshmallowy cloud, like a woolly sheep without legs.

"That's perfect!" Mrs. Harmon beamed at John. "Exactly right for our tapestry. Kobie, your co-artist is very talented, don't you think?"

If she knew what I truly thought, she'd send me to the office so fast my tennis shoes would leave skid marks down the hall.

John grinned at me, obviously thinking I liked his cloud, too. His crooked teeth reminded me of a jack-o'-lantern. I'd hated his smile since the first day he joined our class, the way he looked at me when Mrs. Harmon caught me with the "John Oreo" cartoon. How could the teacher actually prefer John's stupid powderpuff cloud to my artistic Frank Forrester cloud? And to call him my co-artist, as if he had worked on the tapestry all along! It was too much.

I plunked my chalk on the countertop, breaking it in half with the force of my decision. "Mrs. Harmon," I announced. "I quit."

"What are you talking about?" she demanded. "You can't quit. You have to finish that mural."

"John can finish the mural," I said, scooting off the supply cupboard. "I quit. Q-U-I-T, quit!"

"I know how to spell it." Mrs. Harmon's tone bordered on the dangerous. "I don't like your attitude, Kobie Roberts. Your problem is, if you can't be the center of attention, you don't want to be involved at all."

"And your problem is you wouldn't know a decent cloud if you tripped over it!" As soon as the words left my mouth, I knew I had gone too far. Even John Orrin was gaping at me, still clenching the purple chalk.

Mrs. Harmon's face flushed a dull red. "Do you want me to call your mother, Kobie? She's right downstairs. I'm sure she'd want to hear how her daughter is misbehaving and acting like a poor sport."

I wasn't acting at all — I really *was* a poor sport, but who wouldn't be? I had slaved for days on that mural and she ruined the whole thing by picking a country bumpkin to be my co-artist. If she had any sense, she'd realize artists worked *alone*, not in pairs.

But she had me and she knew it. Mrs. Harmon wouldn't have to bother writing a note home — a note that just might get lost on the bus. Or phone my mother to come in for a conference. Not with my mother merely a hop, skip, and a tattle away.

"Well?" She tapped a pencil on the blackboard, waiting for my response.

"I'm sorry," I mumbled, hating the way I had to grovel in front of her when *I* had been wronged.

"Now apologize for disrupting the class."

Actually, the others were delighted by the interruption. Nobody in their right mind was anxious to do social studies. I dutifully apologized to the class.

Mrs. Harmon seemed satisfied. "If you hurry, you and John could have the mural finished by lunch."

"No." I stood firmly by my desk. "I'm not working on the mural anymore."

"Kobie — " she cautioned.

"Mrs. Harmon, I apologized for the things I said, but I meant it about quitting. I'm not working on the project."

The tension between me and my teacher was like a cold steel wire. Nervous perspiration trickled down my backbone. I was petrified. Talking back was bad enough, but I had never defied a teacher in my life. But then, my refusing to work on the mural was small potatoes compared to the stuff Mrs. Harmon had to put up with from Vincent Wheatly and Richard Supinger all the time. Maybe that was why she relented, without sending me to the office or downstairs to my mother.

"If you want to let your classmates down, then that's your business," she said coolly. "John will finish the tapestry. Open your social studies book to page 143."

I sat down, shaking. "I didn't have any choice," I whispered to Gretchen across the aisle. "Look how she messed up my mural by letting John draw my cloud over. You think I did the right thing, don't you?"

"Sure you did," Gretchen said loyally. "You stuck by your principles and that's what counts."

I wasn't sure what principles were involved and I certainly didn't feel as if I had scored any great victory. While I was catching up on all the social studies I had missed the last few weeks, John Orrin was adding the final touches to *my* mural.

My father came home early that evening to finish my tree house. "Might as well use what little daylight we have left before the time goes back," he said.

As he nailed the bannister rails to the staircase, I fooled around the edge of the woods, collecting huge poplar leaves. Except for the railing, the staircase to my tree house had been completed for a week. Every day after school, I'd stand at the bottom of the steps, longing to be hidden among the branches of my very own tree house, but too scared to climb up there.

Gretchen and the others on my bus could see my tree house from the road. "Boy, are you lucky," Gretchen said. "I can't wait to come over and see your tree house."

"It's not quite done yet." I put her off, not wanting her to find out her best friend was really a jellyfish.

So I gathered poplar leaves as big as fans and hoped that my fear of heights would be miraculously cured by the time my father hammered the last nail.

"Okay," he said after a while. "Want to try it out?"

"You're done?" I jumped, scattering the leaves. Zero hour had arrived. Do or die. Looking up the length of the long, long staircase, I decided dying was probably easier than doing.

My father tested the bannisters to demonstrate their sturdiness. "These won't come off in a hurricane. And I made the steps extra-shallow, so you shouldn't be afraid to climb up."

I shouldn't be afraid, but I was. Putting one faltering foot on the bottom step, I said, "Maybe if you weren't watching. . . ."

"I'll be in the shed," he said. "If you need me, just holler."

Gripping the side rails like a drowning man clinging to a life preserver, I slowly crawled up five steps. Then I stopped and looked back to see how high I was. About twelve inches, by my estimation. My father had made the steps shallow, as he said, but the tree house was at least fifteen feet off the ground. My heart thumped, a sure sign I was about to wimp out. Then I remembered what had happened in school earlier. If I could defy my teacher and quit a class project, I could get up those dumb stairs.

My feet carried me up a few more steps. The doorway to the tree house seemed miles away yet. *Don't look down*, I instructed myself, but of course I did. Way, way below me, the poplar leaves I had dropped lay in a yellow puddle. Surprisingly, I didn't feel dizzy.

Gretchen's voice echoed in my head: *You stuck to your principles and that's what counts*. That got me up a couple more steps.

And then I was at the top, swinging

through the doorway into my tree house. The man who scaled Mt. Everest the first time must have felt this great!

I went over to one of the long windows and bravely leaned out. My father was walking back to the shed with his tools. The sun was setting behind him, casting a giant shadow on the path. "I made it!" I yelled. "See? I'm here!"

He turned and touched his cap, saluting my accomplishment. "How do you like it?"

"I love it! Thanks, Dad!"

It was amazing. I didn't mind the height the least bit! Now I could probably do all sorts of high-up things like hang from the monkey bars at school and shinny up the persimmon tree next to my father's shed. A whole new world had opened up to me.

Things looked different from fifteen feet up in the air. Our house appeared to be mostly roof and my father, striding back from his shed, seemed smaller.

Through the red-gold leaves of the oak tree, I gazed at the horizon. The sun was sinking below the distant Blue Ridge mountains, tinting the clouds a hazy pink. I noticed the clouds were neither flat on the bottom with swoopy-scalloped tops nor plump like marshmallows. These clouds were something in between, a shape I couldn't describe.

Chapter 7

Three days later, Gretchen and I saw the old man on the hill for the first time.

We were skipping recess in the Honeysuckle Hideout. I was busy digging up the treasury box because it was Dues Day.

"I think the mural looks awful," I said, furiously shoveling dirt. "The trees and clouds and flowers that John drew are terrible. Mrs. Harmon doesn't have any taste. She thinks John's stuff looks great. I don't even want my name on it now."

"Don't worry about it," Gretchen reassured me. "We'll still win. The castle and the horses you did are so good we have to."

I couldn't let it go. "A medieval tapestry is supposed to have a certain style and that's the way I tried to make it. Those marshmallow clouds and broccoli-stalk trees John put in ruin the whole thing, but do you think Mrs. Harmon cares? No, she just — "

"Kobie!" Gretchen broke in excitedly. "That's him!"

"Who? If John Orrin is sneaking around our hideout again, I'm going to give him what for — " I brandished the digging spoon like a club.

"Not John! The old man on the hill! He just came out of his house!" She gestured for me to get up and look.

I scrambled to my feet. The vines of our hideout were starting to wither, so I only had to separate a few strands to view the house up on the hill. A shambling figure was making its way toward a gray weathered outbuilding. It was the old man, all right. No mistake.

His sparse white hair was fluffed by the breeze, like a dandelion gone to seed. He wore khaki "wash" pants and a plaid shirt. I strained my eyes looking for a telltale hammer or even a screwdriver. He appeared clean from this distance.

"The Hammer Man in the flesh!" I said, awestruck. The legend lived! "On the FBI's Ten-Most-Wanted list and there he is, just walking around his yard like he's perfectly innocent. Little does anyone know how dangerous he really is."

"He doesn't look very dangerous to me,"

Gretchen said. "He looks like an ordinary old man. In fact, I think he's kind of cute, in a grandfatherly sort of way."

I stared at her. "Cute! I suppose you think Frankenstein is cute! And the Werewolf reminds you of a cuddly little puppy! Honestly, Gretch, how dumb can you get?"

"Well, does he look like a murderer to you?"

"Dangerous criminals don't advertise with a big sign, you know. They look like regular people, most of the time." We watched as the Hammer Man reached the outbuilding and fumbled to unlatch the door. "That's actually a clever disguise, going around like somebody's grandfather. People would never suspect who he really is."

"He certainly is slow," Gretchen observed. "I bet he wouldn't hurt a flea."

"All part of his disguise. And it's working. He already has you fooled." I continued my observations, knowing Gretchen was fuming.

"I am not fooled!" she returned, stung by my remark. "You don't know everything, Kobie Roberts. You could be wrong!"

I gave her a smug look that said I was never wrong. And I wasn't — well, hardly ever. I felt it in my bones that the old man with the sweet, white hair and the shuffling gait was in reality the dangerous man who skulked out of Manassas one hot summer night years ago.

Gretchen was still huffy. "If he's so dangerous, then what is he doing in that shed?" The old man had finally disappeared inside and shut the door. "Probably potting geraniums."

"I doubt it." I deepened my voice for effect. "That's where he keeps them. The hammers. The evidence we need to prove who he really is."

"Ohhh, no!" She shook her head, her ponytail lashing back and forth. "I know what you're thinking. I'm not going anywhere near that man's shed. Not in a million years."

"How about for a million *dollars*?" Gretchen had an obstinate streak but, sooner or later, I knew she'd come around.

"What do you mean, a million dollars?"

"Reward money! Gretch, this guy's been at large for ages — I bet the reward money is worth a fortune by now!" I envisioned sacks of coins and mounds of cash piled up like the loot in Scrooge McDuck's money bin. But even more tantalizing, in my mind, was the star-spangled acclaim that came with turning in the Hammer Man. Fame was within our grasp. I had to make Gretchen see that.

She was weakening. "I don't know . . . he seems harmless enough. What if he gets violent?"

"He won't," I told her confidently. "We just have to be smarter than he is. I've got a plan."

"Your last plan almost got us arrested," she said, referring to the Great Indian Pottery Fraud of fifth grade.

Last year, while we were tunneling out the Honeysuckle Hideout, I found some broken crockery. When I suggested we sell the pieces as ancient Indian pottery, Gretchen had to be convinced over and over that we wouldn't get in trouble. Then we went behind the baseball diamond and sold five pieces for a nickel each, before our teacher heard about it. She made us give the kids back their money and told us if we ever tried a hoax like that again, we'd go to jail. Personally, I felt if some kids were gullible enough to believe a piece of a stone crock was really a fragment of Indian pottery, they deserved to lose five cents.

"We didn't almost get arrested," I said, setting the record straight. "Miss Price screamed a lot, but she hardly did anything. It was still a good idea — I almost earned twenty-five cents for the treasury."

Gretchen sighed. "All right. What's your plan?"

"It's really very simple. We wait till he's in the shed — not today, because recess is nearly over. You go up to the door and knock — "

"Me? Why me?"

"Listen to the whole thing before you squawk." I went on, "When he answers, you fall down like you're sick or something. He'll run over to help you and while he's doing that, I'll creep in the shed and grab one of his hammers. When you see me coming out, you get well fast. After I've gone down the hill, you jump up and — "

"How come *I'm* the one who has to pretend to be sick?"

"Because," I said smoothly, "you're a better actress than me. If I pretended to be sick, he'd see right through me in a flash."

"I don't know. . . ." She wasn't quite hooked yet.

Now it was my turn to sigh. These days it was harder and harder to get people to do things. What was the world coming to, when a person could dangle the possibility of a million dollars plus overnight glory, and yet her best friend still wouldn't leap at the chance? Gretchen's assignment was kid's stuff compared to mine. All she had to do was roll around on the ground and gag. *I* had to sneak into the shed, right under the Hammer Man's nose, take one of the murder weapons and any other evidence I could lay my fingers on, then sneak back out before he saw me. Talk about dangerous!

We put our dues in the treasury box and buried it again before the bell rang. I had plenty of time to persuade Gretchen the plan would work. One thing was for sure, the Hammer Man wasn't going anywhere.

Room 11's mural was displayed prominently in the place of honor by the main office when I walked into the school Monday morning. I recognized Lynette O'Bannon's sharp line in the jousting tournament the tapestry illustrated. Room 11's tapestry was very, very good.

Our tapestry was hanging on the wall outside the door to room 10. Whoever had stitched John Orrin's lamb's-wool cloud had made the stitches too loopy. The cloud drooped over the flag-topped tower of my beautiful castle like an old rag. That stupid cloud spoiled the entire mural. No wonder we didn't win.

When the parents came on Back-to-School Night, they'd spot room 11's tapestry first thing because everyone had to go by the office and they'd know that the best artist in the school drew the scene. Only the parents of sixth graders would trudge all the way up the hall to see the mural of the losing class. After taking one look at John Orrin's cloud, they probably wouldn't even want to see the rest of the mural, the parts *I* drew.

Next to the mural, Mrs. Harmon had posted the names of all the students in room 10. Uncapping my pen, I scratched my name off the list. I didn't want the parents to think I had anything to do with that awful tapestry.

As I took my seat, I heard rumbles of discontent over the contest decision from the other kids. Some of them seemed to be aimed in my direction.

"Mr. Magyn said the contest was close," Mrs. Harmon claimed. "He said he wished he had room by the office to hang both tapestries." I didn't believe a word of it. She was only trying to make us feel better.

Kathy Stall prodded me with her pencil. "It's your fault we lost," she hissed. "You quit and made us lose."

"My fault!" I couldn't believe the nerve of that girl. "You were the one who griped about my cloud. If you hadn't opened your mouth, I would have finished the mural."

Marcia Dittier twisted around. "Your cloud was dumb. I'm glad Mrs. Harmon got somebody else to do it over. But you shouldn't have quit."

"I had to quit," I said, thinking that Vincent Wheatly should have chopped off the rest of Marcia's ugly hair. "The idea was, *one* person would draw the mural. And that person was me. You voted for me, so you ought to know."

"That was before we found out you took art lessons from the weatherman." Kathy cackled at her own stupid joke.

I thought how wonderful Kathy Stall would look staked to an anthill.

"Quitter, quitter, quit-ter," Kathy chanted. "Kobie Robert's a quitter!" To my delight Mrs. Harmon wryly asked her which she'd rather do, pay attention to fractions or take a little walk to the office? Kathy shushed, but from time to time she and Marcia would sing in voices no one but me could hear, "Quitter, quitter, quit-ter!"

I sensed a chilliness in the room. The whole class was blaming me for losing the competition. I could feel it.

It was worse at recess. Vincent Wheatly and Richard Supinger cornered Gretchen and me on the playground before we could escape to the Honeysuckle Hideout. Kathy and Marcia and some other kids joined them.

Richard grabbed my arm. "You blew it, Roberts."

I rubbed my arm, scanning the blacktop

for Mrs. Harmon. She was busy setting up a four-square game. "I didn't blow anything. It wasn't my fault Mr. Magyn liked room 11's mural better. You can't blame me."

"You dropped out," Vincent jeered. "If you'd finished it instead of running off like a baby, we would've won."

Gretchen sprang to my defense. "Kobie did more work than anybody on that project. Don't you dare say it's her fault."

"It *is* her fault," Richard stated flatly. Vincent agreed. You couldn't argue with those two. They ran room 10 with their big mouths and their big muscles and nothing Gretchen could say would make any difference.

"Come on," I told her, hoping the boys would let us go if we just walked past them.

Vincent shoved me into Richard. "Where's the quitter going?"

"Probably down to those bushes she likes so much," Kathy taunted.

Vincent stood on the toes of my tennis shoes so I couldn't budge. Richard Supinger pinned Gretchen's arms behind her back.

"Leave us alone," I yelled. "Or I'll tell the teacher!"

"Tattletale, tattletale, hang your pants

on a rusty nail!" Vincent sang, wiggling his eyebrows. He had funny little peaked eyebrows and eyelashes so blond they were almost white. When I doodled cartoons of Vincent Wheatly, I made his eyes oblong and blank like Little Orphan Annie's.

"Shut up, Whitey," I said, daringly calling him a name I knew he despised. One way to get them off the subject of the mural was to make them mad about something else.

Vincent reacted instantly, twisting the material of my jacket around his fist. "What did you call me?"

Gretchen pulled away from Richard and ran over to Mrs. Harmon. As soon as the boys saw where she was heading, they let me go, pushing me so hard I fell on the blacktop and scraped my knee. I just lay there, holding my knee and blinking back tears. I could see Gretchen telling Mrs. Harmon what had happened, pointing at Vincent and Richard, who were down on the softball field acting as if they'd been there for hours.

Mrs. Harmon ordered me to the nurse's office to get patched up. She let Gretchen go with me. I hobbled back into the building, blood dribbling down my leg and into my sock.

"Vincent and Richard are in for it now," Gretchen consoled me. "They'll be sorry they knocked you down."

"No, they won't. They'll probably do it again." At the water fountain I wet a tissue and wiped most of the blood off my leg.

"They're bullies," she said. "You can't expect them to behave like normal human beings."

"It's not just them. It's everybody in the whole class. They hate me, Gretchen, I know they do. They hate me because I quit the project and our mural lost."

For once, she didn't say anything and I knew she thought I was right about the class hating me. Maybe she hated me, too.

"You don't blame me, do you?" I said, almost crying. If my best friend turned against me, I couldn't stand it. "You don't think it's my fault?"

She found a used tissue in her pocket and handed it to me. "Of course I don't blame you, Kobie. You did the best you could. Mrs. Harmon should have let you finish the project the way you wanted."

There wasn't anybody else around. I let the tears flow, not caring that Gretchen was watching, not caring that I was going on twelve, too old to cry. I should have been the Best Artist in Centreville Elementary.

Instead, the others thought I was the Benedict Arnold of room 10. There was only one way I could redeem myself — I absolutely *had* to discover the true identity of the Hammer Man. If I helped the police capture a dangerous criminal, everybody would forget about the stupid mural contest.

"Somebody's coming," Gretchen murmured.

I stopped sniveling. It sounded like only a kid coming down the hall, but I didn't want anybody to see me bawling. My reputation was already a disaster.

Gretchen peeked around the corner. "Don't worry. It's just John Orrin."

He clumped down the hall, evidently on an errand for Mrs. Harmon. He smiled as he went by, then said, idiotically, "Your leg's bleeding, Kobie."

"No kidding," I said stonily.

My heart hardened like a lump of coal. It wasn't my fault at all that our class lost the contest. It was *John's*. His dumb puffy cloud ruined our mural. *He* should have been the one Vincent pushed on the blacktop, not me.

John always managed to get off scot-free, while I always got dumped on. Thanks to John, Mrs. Harmon chewed me out over the "John Oreo" cartoon. Thanks to John,

I was forced to quit the project. Thanks to John, our class lost the contest. Everything was John Orrin's fault, yet I was the one taking the blame.

Well, that was about to change, I decided, anticipating the sting of iodine the nurse would swab on my knee. Starting tomorrow, John Orrin was going to pay me back.

Chapter 8

I licked the tip of my pencil and scribbled faster, trying to finish my one-page science report before the bus came. Mrs. Harmon was making us give our reports orally, so my writing didn't have to be that great. This report was super-important. Not for my grade, but for the beginning of the downfall of John Orrin.

From the doorway of my tree house, I could see at least a quarter of a mile down Lee Highway. I'd be able to spot the blunt yellow snout of the bus as it cruised over the hill and still have plenty of time to gather my books and run down to the stop, where my mother was standing alone.

I had fixed my tree house up really cool. A sign on one of the braces warned away trespassers: *Abandon Hope All Ye Who Enter.* My mother had donated a plastic shower curtain set and her old tin kitchen cannisters. With my father's help, I covered the roof with the shower curtain. On rainy days, I could let down the sides of the curtain over the windows. I put little things in the cannisters — small notebooks, pencils, even candy. The cannisters had tight lids that kept squirrels out.

My father gave me a three-legged wooden footstool and an old bunch of keys on a ring. The keys didn't go to anything, but I liked the solid "house" look of keys hanging on a peg. My father said those great big keys gave my place more of a jailhouse look.

Because I didn't like it down in the basement anymore, I moved my ancient encyclopedias to my tree house, covering the heavy books with the plastic window curtain that came with the shower curtain set. The books came in handy when I had to whip up a quick report, like today.

For science, though, the old encyclopedias were kind of a hindrance. Gretchen was doing her report on dinosaurs. I couldn't even find dinosaurs in my encyclopedia, which made me wonder how old the books really *were*. Having learned my lesson not to trust the astronomy section in the Science volume, I stuck to the safer subject of Animals, deciding to do my report on a toad with scaly trapdoors in its skin, where it carries its babies. No one else in room 10 would write about trap-door toads, I was sure.

Trying to describe the toad in my own words was hard. You had to *see* this toad to understand how the trapdoors worked, how the tiny baby toads hold up their own little doors like sewer workers lifting up manhole covers. I filled half of my one page report with an illustration. But Mrs. Harmon didn't like reports with drawings anymore than she liked long division problems answered but not worked out, so I had to write a few paragraphs. Somebody ought to tell that woman that a picture is worth a thousand words.

Already I'd run into a problem. According to my encyclopedia, trap-door toads lived in Italian West Africa. Even I was aware no such country existed anymore, but since I didn't know what the new name was, I had to leave it.

"Bus!" somebody shouted.

Forgetting where I was for an instant, I looked up in surprise to see my mother waving at me to hurry up, the bus was coming. The way she yelled "Bus!" startled me. She could have been a kid. There's always someone who dawdles and someone who tells other kids to get moving.

I stuffed my report in my notebook and

trotted down the steps. I made it just as the bus was pulling up.

"Your hair is a mess," my mother commented, swiping at my bangs with one hand. The illusion that she might be a regular kid waiting for the bus burst like a soap bubble. She was only my mother, a horrible embarrassment I had to endure, like a bad case of hives.

Gretchen didn't know I was out to get John Orrin. When she sat next to me on the bus, I resisted telling her about my plan and instead showed her my illustrated report.

"Look at those tiny frogs coming out of the warts!" she squealed. "Kobie, what a gruesome picture!"

"They aren't frogs," I explained patiently. "They're toads. And those bumps aren't warts, but little trapdoors the babies live in to stay safe. Isn't it neat?"

Gretchen let me read her copied-over-three-times report on the brontosaurus. I stared at her neat, round handwriting, in reality thinking about the little trap I was going to set for a certain warty toad named John Orrin.

At school while the others were milling around and talking before the late bell, I dropped my notebook right in front of John's desk. Papers fluttered all over the place. I got down on my hands and knees to pick them up. When nobody was paying attention, I crammed my science report in the cubbyhole under John's desk.

As usual, slowpoke John was the last kid to take his seat. He stowed his books under his desk without ever noticing the piece of paper that didn't belong there. I stifled a snicker. In an hour or so, John would probably be expelled. Or at the very least ordered to the principal for a good bawling out.

Mrs. Harmon preferred to start oral reports right away, so the students wouldn't have to agonize all day about getting up in front of the class, a policy she instituted after Danny Blevins threw up on the world globe. Danny said he felt sick waiting to give his report.

Our one-page science reports were supposed to last three minutes. Mine wouldn't take that long, since it was mostly picture, but it didn't matter. After the ruckus was over, Mrs. Harmon would probably forget all about making me give my report.

For obvious reasons, Danny Blevins was called on first. Then Marcia Dittier, who giggled through her presentation, and then Vincent Wheatly, who told Mrs. Harmon his cat had her kittens on his report and he couldn't move her. The whole class cracked up at this original excuse. Mrs. Harmon pursed her lips and marked a zero in the grade book.

"Kobie Roberts," she called.

I clasped my hands on my desk and tried to make my face blank.

"Come up here, Kobie," Mrs. Harmon said, still irritated over Vincent Wheatly's excuse. "We haven't got all day."

"I can't," I told her solemnly.

"Why can't you?" she demanded. "Didn't you do your report, either?"

"Yes, ma'am." I hadn't said "ma'am" in so long, the word tasted funny in my mouth, like water sitting overnight in the bottom of a glass.

Mrs. Harmon ruffled her curly hair, exasperated. "Then get up here, Kobie! We're waiting."

"I can't."

She sighed. "I thought you said you did your report."

"I did."

Mrs. Harmon enunciated every word carefully, as if I had suddenly grown stupid. "Do you or do you not have your science report?"

"She probably quit in the middle like she did with the mural," Richard Supinger said.

Everybody in the class still blamed me for losing the mural contest. Only Gretchen treated me like a normal person. The others either snubbed me or else picked on me constantly.

"Be quiet, Richard," Mrs. Harmon barked, her patience just about gone, "unless you want a zero alongside your name, too. Kobie, if you're not up here in two seconds with your report — "

"I wrote my report, Mrs. Harmon," I said, "but I don't have it."

"If you left it at home, that's the same as not doing it and you get a zero."

I spoke up before she marked a goose egg beside my name in the grade book. "I didn't leave it at home. *He's* got it and he won't give it back." Standing up dramatically like a witness in a courtroom drama, I pointed at John Orrin.

John's face crumpled in shock, too stunned to deny my accusation.

"Kobie, I would like to get through science before midnight," Mrs. Harmon said wearily. "Why does John have your report?"

"He took it," I lied. "He took it away from me so I'd get a bad grade."

"John, is this true?"

John worked his mouth like a gasping

fish. At last he managed to say, "Mrs. Harmon, I don't know nothing about Kobie's report."

"She says you took it." Mrs. Harmon whirled on me again. "Kobie, when did John take your report?"

I hadn't thought that far ahead. "This morning. Before the late bell." I remembered that Mrs. Harmon had been out of the room then, talking to Mrs. Wright across the hall.

She looked at me dubiously, reluctant to believe her pet was capable of such a spiteful deed, then said, "John, give Kobie her report."

"I don't have it!" he cried. "I never saw no report! She's — " He stopped and stared at me. I knew what he'd been about to say, that I was lying.

I glared back at him, determined not to buckle under even though I was lying through my teeth. My entire future in room 10 depended on pulling this off. "If you don't believe *me*, Mrs. Harmon," I said with an injured sniff, "go through his desk. That's where he put it. Under his books."

Mrs. Harmon made John take his books out one by one. When he pulled out my trapdoor toad report, he gaped as if he'd been caught with the floor plan to the National Bank of Virginia.

"I don't know how this got in my desk," he stuttered.

Mrs. Harmon delivered the wadded-up report to me, her eyes flashing. I couldn't tell if she was annoyed by the delay or if she suspected I had set the whole thing up. As it turned out, John wasn't expelled or even sent to the office and I got a "C—" on my presentation because I had drawn a picture instead of writing a full page.

Gretchen gawked at me when I sat down again. I knew she had figured out the truth. She passed a scrap of paper torn from her notebook with a single question mark on it. I didn't answer her note, too busy plotting my next move.

At recess, Gretchen headed for the Honeysuckle Hideout, but I pulled her into a dodgeball game instead.

"Kobie, what — ?" she asked as I found two spaces in the circle.

"I want to play this for a change."

It wasn't easy getting into the game. On my other side, Kathy and Marcia jostled me, but I held firm. John Orrin was the last one on the blacktop. He stood timidly at the edge of the circle, waiting for Rack Carter to chuck the ball to him. The object of the game was to strike a person in the center of the ring. Then you got to trade places with them, and dodge other people's throws. John didn't even try to hit anyone, but one of the kids in the middle got in the way of the ball, so John got to take his place.

When the ball bounced over to me, I hefted its weight. John watched me steadily, but didn't flinch when I pretended to throw the ball. I threw again, this time with all my might, hoping to wallop him a good one. I was a rotten thrower, unable to hit the side of a parked tractor-trailer, much less a moving target, but I struck John's arm with a glancing blow. John was a rotten player. He stayed outside the circle, feebly tossing the ball and missing everyone, until Gretchen stepped in the way of his throw.

With a defiant glance at me, she exchanged places with John. Because I didn't want to hit my best friend when the ball came into my hands again, I deliberately missed her. Then I caught Danny Blevins on the elbow with the ball and took his place in the circle.

But when I saw the looks on the other kids' faces, I realized it wasn't the safest place to be. They creamed me, pelting me with fast, hard throws that didn't let up until Mrs. Harmon blew her whistle.

Gretchen avoided speaking to me until

we were sitting at our table in the lunch-room.

"What's with you, Kobie?" she asked. "John never took your science report."

I bit happily into my Vienna sausage sandwich, mayonnaise spurting up between the neatly sliced meat. "I know. I made it up."

She was aghast. "But why? You almost got him in trouble with the teacher. What's he ever done to you?"

"What's he done to me? Plenty, that's what! He got Mrs. Harmon mad at me the first day he came. And then he had to horn in on the mural project and cause us to lose the contest. It's all John's fault nobody in our class likes me. I'm just paying him back."

Gretchen twirled her fork in her mashed potatoes, breaking the dam so gravy leaked into the Swiss steak. "I don't see how being mean to John will make the kids like you again."

It was difficult to explain. For one reason, everybody liked Gretchen. She'd never experienced the humiliation of having kids squirt her at the water fountain, knock her over on the playground, or make snide remarks in the halls. The other reason was that I wasn't too sure it would work. Picking on John Orrin might make the other kids hate me even worse. But that was a risk I'd have to take. Maybe, just maybe, they'd think I was a big shot and I'd *be* somebody again in room 10.

"It's the only thing left for me to do," I said. "Gretchen, there's something about that kid that drives me crazy. He's always so . . . calm. Even when he was getting clobbered in recess today, he just stood there like a ninny. He brought all this on himself."

"Your favorite person is heading this way. The other tables must be full again."

John Orrin! Coming to sit at our table after all that had happened this morning! The kid was either calmer than I imagined or unbelievably stupid.

"Howdy," he drawled. "Okay if I sit here?"

I shrugged, knowing I had no choice, not with the lunchroom warden monitoring us. Still, I could tell John was uneasy sitting next to me.

"Good lunch today," he said, tucking his napkin in his belt. "What's this?" He dunked his spoon into the little dish of fruit.

"Mandarin oranges," Gretchen said. "You've never had mandarin oranges before?"

"Actually," I spoke up, "they're dead goldfish."

John goggled at me. "Goldfish?"

I was on a roll. "Yes, the cafeteria ladies pull off the little fins so you can't tell. You eat them whole — they slide right down. If you chew them, you'll crunch up — "

"Kobie, will you stop?!" Gretchen admonished. To John she said, "Kobie always does this during lunch."

"Not just lunch," I said to no one in particular. I wanted John to realize that I was after him, if he didn't already know it.

"About this morning," Gretchen said suddenly. "That mix-up over Kobie's report? It was just a joke, John. Kobie's a terrible kidder."

"Oh, it was a *joke*!" John's face split into a smile, as if we had given him an unexpected present. "Like the goldfish. Boy, you really had me going for a while," he admitted to me.

I wanted to throttle Gretchen. How could I ever get even with John Orrin when she had him thinking I was the class clown?

"You took it pretty good," Gretchen said, still on the subject of my "joke." "Most kids would tell the teacher."

"I couldn't do that," John said. "If it

was only a joke, why get Kobie in trouble? Right, Kobie?"

He regarded me with his watery gray eyes, calm as a pond on a summer's day, and smiled. He had me and he knew it.

I hastily revised my opinion of John Orrin. He wasn't stupid at all. He was actually quite smart, knowing all along the mandarin oranges weren't goldfish and managing to reduce my clever trap to a crude sixth-grade prank. If I was going to regain my self-esteem in room 10 by waging war on John Orrin, I had my work cut out for me.

Chapter 9

My life suddenly became very busy.

Every morning, I had to check the seat of my desk for bubble gum. Whenever I went up to the front of the class to sharpen my pencil, I had to pry a chipped piece of lead out of the sharpener that always seemed to be there. Broken lead would only gnaw my pencil to a nubbin instead of sharpening it. The back of my jacket often had a "Kick Me" sign taped to it and once I came in from recess to find one of my best drawings, a Halloween cat, tampered with. Someone, probably Kathy Stall, had scrawled a stuck-out tongue and a cartoon balloon over my cat's head with the caption, "Kobie Roberts is a stinker."

The kids — at least four of them — were still blaming me for losing that stupid mural contest.

When I wasn't heading off possible sabotage, I watched out the window to catch the Hammer Man going out to his shed. Gretchen and I planned to put our fake-sickness scheme into action the next recess period we knew the Hammer Man was out of the house.

In between, I did a little schoolwork. My first-six-weeks report card was dismal, "D"s in arithmetic, science, and social studies. Under "Growth and Participation," the section where teachers loved to snitch on kids, Mrs. Harmon gave me the lowest mark for "Uses Time Wisely" and "Gets Along Well With Others." My folder of "A" papers my parents had to ooh and aah over on Back-to-School Night was pitifully scanty.

But mostly I was busy trying to get even with John Orrin.

He was driving me crazy! *Nothing* I did to him seemed to faze his maddening calmness. If I accidentally-on-purpose tripped him as he was coming down the aisle, *he'd* apologize to *me* for stepping on *my* foot! When I told him I'd never seen hair the color of his before, he took it as a compliment. Another time I commented on his too-short pants, asking him if he was expecting a flood and he laughed as if this was the funniest thing he'd ever heard. He never whined the day I threw spitballs at him, even when one landed in his ear, and he didn't tattle when I tore his history essay almost in half and he had to copy it over.

"I can't shake that kid no matter what I do," I said to Gretchen as we did our homework over the phone one evening.

"Kobie, why don't you leave him alone?" she said. "He's not hurting you."

"He is, too! He's the cause of my troubles at school. Nobody would be picking on me if John had stayed wherever he came from. It's all his fault."

"I still don't see how picking on John will make the other kids stop picking on *you*." Sometimes I hated the way Gretchen was always so logical, but that was probably why she understood fractions and long division and I didn't.

"If I could beat John *just once*, the others will know I'm a — a force to be reckoned with." I borrowed that phrase from an old movie I had seen the other night.

"I don't like it," Gretchen said. "I don't like it when somebody picks on another kid."

"What do you think Richard and Kathy and Vincent and the others are doing to *me*?" I flung back.

"It's different because you aren't by yourself. John doesn't have any friends."

True, but it didn't change the way I felt

about him one bit. Then I began to wonder
if Gretchen was trying to tell me something
without coming right out and saying it.

"Will you still be my friend?" I asked.
"Even if I keep after John?"

Her sigh hummed through the phone
wires. "I'll always be your friend, Kobie,
even when you do things I don't like."

That was a relief. Without Gretchen, I
wouldn't have the strength to face those
hostile kids in room 10 day after day. Of
course John didn't have any friends, but
that was his own tough luck, barging into
class so late in the year after everybody
had already paired off.

"You know," Gretchen mused. "John
isn't so bad, if you'd just talk to him. Why
don't you bury the hatchet and try to be
friends?"

"Friends with *John*? Gretchen, are you
delirious?"

"Well, maybe not be a friend-friend,"
she backed down. "But would it be so terrible if he ate lunch with us?"

"That's the only time we have to ourselves except recess." Next, she'd want to
invite him into our hideout.

"It's just a suggestion, Kobie. Sometimes
it gets a little lonesome at lunch, just you
and me."

"How can it be lonesome? I'm there. Who else do you need?" Years ago, we decided not to include anyone else in our group. I liked being exclusive. "We have a lot more fun than those other girls," I said. "Don't we?"

"I guess so." Gretchen's voice seemed thin.

The next morning, I jumped into my clothes and ran out to the kitchen. Dressed in her cafeteria uniform, my mother was jotting down a list and enjoying a last cup of coffee.

Before I put a fingernail on the cabinet handle, she said, "You have to buy lunch today, Kobie. There's nothing here to make your lunch out of until I get to the store."

"Buy my lunch!" I shrieked, as if she just said she'd enrolled me in sword-swallowing lessons. "I can't do that! I never buy my lunch." At least, not since she started working at my school.

She finished the list and put it in her purse. "Well, you'll have to suffer today and buy. I told you we don't have anything in the house."

"Why don't we? What kind of a mother are you, not buying groceries when you're supposed to?" She didn't realize what she was making me do, go through *her* serving line, when my reputation in sixth grade was already floundering.

"This is a house, not a restaurant," she said tersely. "And it's not run to suit you, missy. I don't want to hear anymore back talk, do you hear?"

I changed my tune in a hurry. Feverishly rummaging through the cupboards, I found the end of a loaf of bread, a jar of mustard, and a few stale Fritos.

"Look! There's plenty of stuff here," I sang out. "I can make — a mustard-and-Fritos sandwich! I love Fritos and mustard!"

"I'm sure you do, but that's hardly a nutritious combination." Working in a cafeteria had given my mother all sorts of notions about what a person should eat.

"Okay, you want vitamins . . . how's this?" I flourished a shriveled apple from the crisper in the refrigerator. The apple was so old my fingers sunk into the mealy flesh. Ordinarily I wouldn't even touch a piece of fruit that gross, much less consider eating it, but I was desperate.

"Throw that nasty thing in the garbage," my mother said. "And take your lunch money. You're buying and that's final."

"I'll starve first! I don't want to go through your old line!" I was on the verge of crying again. My father wouldn't have been so mean to me. He would have driven me to George's Store to buy a pre-made sandwich or let me fix whatever I wanted. But he wasn't here and my mother was.

She got up and came over to me, ominous in her spanking-white uniform and rubber-soled shoes. Anger sparked her dark brown eyes. "I've had enough out of you for one morning, Kobie Roberts. You don't think I can't make you eat your lunch? What if I jerked you up and dragged you through the lunch line, right in front of everybody? What if I stood over you and made you eat? What if I *fed* you, like a little baby?"

She'd do it, too. I had pushed her as far as she was going to be pushed. Snatching up my lunch money, I ran out the door without another word.

When lunchtime arrived, I walked very slowly down to the cafeteria.

"How come you're so poky today?" Gretchen asked. "I'm starving."

"Go on," I urged. "I have to buy and I want to make sure I'm last in line."

"Are you still down on your mother because she works here? Honestly, Kobie, nobody really cares whether your mother hands you your lunch or not."

"You don't know my mother, Gretch. She'll make a scene today, I just know it.

We had a big hairy fight this morning and she's going to get even with me." I loitered down the stairs, placing both feet on each step to take longer to reach the bottom.

"Kobie, mothers don't get even with their kids. You've got revenge on the brain lately. I don't know what's the matter with you." Disgusted, she went ahead without me.

I managed to be the very last one in line, right behind — who else? — John Orrin.

John selected his flatware with exaggerated care, as if he were having lunch at a fancy restaurant instead of our dumpy old cafeteria, placing his knife and fork and spoon squarely on his napkin. Behind him, I impatiently snatched a handful from the bins, winding up with four knives and one spoon, slinging the cutlery on my tray with a noisy clatter.

At the milk cooler, John took two milks, then offered one to me. I was so outraged at his nerve — handing me a milk as if we were buddies — that I leaned in and got a *chocolate* milk, knowing perfectly well kids on free lunch weren't permitted to have chocolate milk.

Actually, I wasn't permitted to have chocolate milk, either. As soon as my mother saw the brown carton on my tray, she flew up like a skyrocket. Pushing back a tendril of hair that had escaped her hair net, her cheeks flushed from working over the steam tables, she said, "Put that back right this instant and get regular milk! What have I told you about eating too much junk?"

I could have died of shame. I slunk back to the cooler and swapped the chocolate milk for regular.

John crowed, "Oh, we're having turkey today! Can I have a little extra dressing, Mrs. Roberts?"

My mother smiled at him. "You certainly may, John. I'm giving you extra turkey, too. Eat it all, now."

"Yes, ma'am!" He accepted his plate so eagerly you would have thought it was Baked Alaska rather than the tired old turkey and dressing the school always dished up when they were getting ready to clean out the freezer. "You're the best cook."

I was thoroughly nauseated. John's Oliver Twist act had my mother fawning all over him, but it didn't fool me a bit. How dare he con my mother into giving him extras? Yet if she took requests from him, I might as well put in mine.

"No peas for me today," I said airily to my mother.

"You're getting peas and you're going to eat them." She thrust a plate at me positively brimming with the hateful little green things.

I slammed the plate on my tray and shoved it up the line. John was waiting for me.

"You're mother's nice," he said. "Sometimes she lets me have two rolls."

"Bully for you." It was bad enough going through the serving line behind John — being in the same *country* was too much, really — but to have him smugly tell me the favors my mother granted him, *my mother*, was the absolute limit.

We had reached the cashier's desk by now. John was about to pick up his tray and leave the line when I suddenly yelled, "Where's your MONEY, John? You can't go through without PAYING."

Mrs. Settinger, the cafeteria manager and money-taker, glowered at me. "Go on through," she told John.

"He didn't PAY!" I bellowed. "How come HE doesn't have to pay and I have to? Here's MY dollar! John, where's YOUR DOLLAR?"

John looked as if he wanted to fall through the floor. "I — I — " he stammered painfully.

"It's all right," Mrs. Settinger reassured him. "Go sit down." John grabbed his tray and fled.

"But he didn't PAY!" My throat hurt from yelling so much.

"If you don't keep quiet, you're going to the principal," Mrs. Settinger said menacingly.

I fished four quarters from my pocket. "I didn't want him to get away without paying," I said with mock concern. "My mother says you have to watch some of these kids."

"Yes, you do." Mrs. Settinger dropped the coins into her cash box with a resounding clunk. "I know one kid I'd like to watch getting the tar whaled out of her."

Of course I knew who she meant. As I carried my tray back to our special table, I passed John Orrin sitting by himself, hunched miserably over his lunch. I felt guilt wash over me.

"What was *that* all about?" Gretchen asked.

"You'd have to be there to understand." I didn't feel good about what I had done, but it was over and there wasn't anything I could do about it.

However, someone else could. Mrs. Harmon stalked over to our table and said in a clipped voice, "Three minutes to eat, Kobie, then to the office."

I managed to choke down a few bites of

dry turkey before my time was up. "I wish you could come with me."

"I do, too." Gretchen stared at me with big scared eyes, probably wondering when she'd ever see me again.

The office was empty of other kids on Death Row when I slipped through the door. Behind the counter Miss Warren was pecking at her typewriter, undoubtedly typing a form of some kind. "Yes?" she inquired.

"I'm supposed to see Mr. Magyn."

"Have a seat." She went back to her typing.

This was only the second time I had actually been sent to the office, despite numerous threats from my teachers. Last year I popped a milk carton in the lunchroom and the monitor sent me upstairs. I waited an eternity, dying a thousand deaths, before Mr. Magyn summoned me to his inner office. He asked me my name and what awful thing I had done, then told me not to do it again and let me go back to class. I had a feeling I wouldn't get off so easy today.

I sat on the edge of the vinyl couch. My palms were sweaty. How long would he make me wait? Didn't he know that kids got awfully nervous when they had to wait for the principal? I might even throw up on his globe, the way Danny Blevins did.

At last Miss Warren told me Mr. Magyn would see me. I walked into the inner office with trembling knees. Mr. Magyn sat behind his form-littered desk.

"Sit down, Kobie," he said. A bad sign. He already knew my name, which meant he was probably going to expel me. Then the door opened and my mother came in! I wouldn't even get a chance to clear out my desk; my mother was going to take me straight home. Or to Juvenile Hall.

"Mrs. Roberts," Mr. Magyn greeted her as if we were at a tea party. "Please have a seat."

My mother took the chair next to me. "I'm sorry it took me so long," she apologized. "I had to finish on the line."

"That's quite all right. Kobie needed time to think about her behavior in the lunchroom."

"I'm so ashamed of you, Kobie," my mother said. "Humiliating that boy the way you did! What's gotten into you?"

Mr. Magyn interrupted. "Kobie, you know why you're here. Is there anything you'd like to say?"

"No, sir," I mumbled.

"Why did you do it?" my mother asked.

"Knowing that poor boy is on free lunch, why did you embarrass him that way? You *know* better!"

Yes, I knew John Orrin and all his brothers and sisters were on free lunch and I knew *better*, but I couldn't explain to her in a zillion years what happened on the serving line.

Mr. Magyn leaned forward. "How do you think John felt, Kobie, when you made such a fuss over his not paying?"

"Awful." But, then, so did *I*, yet nobody seemed to care about me.

"What do you think you should do?"

"Pay for his next lunch?" Maybe a little humor would lighten things up.

The principal frowned. Now he was really angry. "Do you think this is funny, Kobie?"

"No," I said lamely. "Sir."

"Usually I like to make the punishment fit the crime. You should be made to apologize to John Orrin at the top of your lungs, the way you humiliated him, in public. But that would only draw more attention to the boy's unfortunate situation." It wouldn't have done much for *my* unfortunate situation, either, but for once I kept quiet.

"I want to see you in my office tomorrow morning at eight-thirty," he continued.

"You will apologize to John Orrin and you will mean it." I nodded. "Also, I want you to write five hundred times in your best handwriting, 'I will not shout in the cafeteria.' Your sentences are due on my desk by noon tomorrow."

In the main office, my mother let me have it. "I was never so embarrassed in my whole life! Hearing that fracas on the line and then having to come up here! You think you got off the hook, apologizing to that boy and writing a few sentences, but just wait till I tell your father when he comes home tonight."

I could stand hearing my mother yell because I was used to it. If she got mad at me, it was no big deal. But I couldn't bear to have my father know what I did. He might tear down my tree house or prevent me from trick-or-treating with Gretchen next Sunday night. But mainly, I didn't want him to find out that going on twelve was making me into a terrible person.

Chapter 10

My mother didn't tell my father what I did, for some reason, but she wouldn't let me write my sentences in my tree house, either. She said it was too cold to sit up there half the evening.

So I stayed in my room with the door shut, writing "I will not shout in the cafeteria." When I finished, hours later, the sentences covered both sides of ten sheets of lined notebook paper.

The next day was more torturous than writing those stupid sentences. In the principal's office, I muttered an apology to John Orrin, who seemed as uncomfortable as I was.

"Kobie is genuinely sorry," Mr. Magyn emphasized. "I hope you two can be friends after this."

I really *was* sorry! But, still, it was all John's fault I said those things in the first place! If he hadn't gushed all over my mother, like she was *his* mother, I wouldn't have made such a scene. No way could I ever be friends with him. Never in a thousand million years.

We went back to class together, but I walked on the opposite side of the hall. He didn't speak. He didn't have to — he'd won and we both knew it.

At least it was library day. Gretchen and I secured a private table by the window, hidden by the nonfiction bookshelves. Gretchen didn't grill me about my ordeal in the principal's office — she was that kind of a friend. She read me silly riddles from this book, like What did the baby chick say when he found an orange in his mother's nest? Oh, look at the orange marmalade!

Soon we were giggling over jokes even dumber than that one.

"I need a drink of water," I gasped. "I'm getting a little hoarse."

"Hope you've got a little hay," Gretchen quipped. "Whinny-whinny, neigh-neigh, nicker-nicker." She was reciting an old gag we started years ago when Lori Bass, who was playing a horse in a puppet show, pronounced her lines phonetically, instead of making horse sounds.

It was really great having a friend like

Gretchen. She always cheered me up when I was down.

"If everything was just like now," I said after our laughter subsided, "we wouldn't need the Hammer Man. I mean, it wouldn't matter if we were famous or not. It would just be you and me having fun."

"I know." Then she said, "Kobie, why don't we forget about this Hammer Man business?"

For a second, I wished we could. I wasn't as brave as I let on — sneaking into a murderer's shed to steal evidence wasn't my idea of fun. But the other kids in room 10 were still on my case. They wouldn't quit until I either moved away or did something heroic.

"We can't forget him," I declared. "The very next time we see him go out to his shed, we'll nab him."

"He never leaves his house. We've only seen him go to his shed once when we were in the Honeysuckle Hideout."

"He'll go out there again." I glanced out the window at his shuttered house. The barren trees and dead grass made the place look even more forbidding.

"It's almost November," she pointed out. "If we didn't see him when the weather was nice, why should we see him when it's practically winter?"

"You have to think positively, Gretch. Let's send him a thought message: Hammer Man, go to your shed. Maybe if we both concentrate hard enough, he'll do it." I was starting to believe the power of my own imagination, visualizing the Hammer Man sleepwalking to his shed, arms outstretched as if he had no control over his body.

We closed our eyes so we could communicate better. But instead of willing the Hammer Man to leave his house, I thought about how my wonderful year was turning out so crummy. I lost the mural contest, forfeiting the title Best Artist in Centreville Elementary (yet I knew I really *was*). I hadn't found my father's King Neptune paper, the one he received when he crossed the equator. So far I hadn't done anything to make a name for myself. At the end of the year I'd be promoted to junior high (maybe) and no one would remember me, even though I had spent six whole years in this school. Kobie *who*?

Gretchen was right about one thing. Winter was coming, which meant indoor recess, stupid stuff like square dancing and sing-alongs. No more running down to the Honeysuckle Hideout to get away from the nerds in our class until spring. If everyone continued to berate me for losing the contest, I didn't know how I'd survive being cooped up with them day after day.

"I can't sit here with my eyes closed," Gretchen said, breaking the silence. She leafed through the mystery book she had picked to check out for the week. "I bet I've read this before."

"I bet you haven't read *this*." Mrs. Sharp glided over to our table and handed Gretchen a magazine article. "Remember that treasure story I promised you? Well, I finally remembered to bring it in."

We pounced on the article, spreading the pages so we both could read it at the same time. It was the greatest treasure story ever, about the Lost Dutchman Mine in the Superstition Mountains in Arizona. Apparently a Dutch prospector in the Wild West days found this gold mine hidden in the desert mountains. He etched coded directions to the mine on stone tablets. Then he died in his mine, too greedy to leave his gold.

Years later, the tablets were discovered and people were searching for the Dutchman's mine. The article told about one prospector whose campsite kept getting wrecked and who even claimed he'd been shot at. He believed it was the ghost of the old Dutchman, back from the dead to drive people away from his mine. Gretchen shivered as she read that paragraph.

"Look at those tablets," I said, referring to the photographs that accompanied the story. "It's like a treasure map."

The granite tablets were tombstone-shaped, with faint markings carved into the surface, arrows and double lines and strange symbols. But the prospector who owned the tablets didn't want people reading the magazine to decipher the code and go busting out to Arizona to find his mine, so he made the magazine photographer put pieces of black tape over the important clues on the tablets.

"I wish we could go out there and find that mine." I was already dreaming about how famous I'd be if I discovered a mine that had been lost for a hundred years and was cursed by a ghost besides.

"We'd never figure out where it was," Gretchen said. "Not without the clues under the tape. Anyway, I'm not too anxious to tangle with a ghost."

"Still, it'd be so neat. If we went out there, all we'd need is some camping equipment and this article."

We talked about the story, rereading parts of the article out loud to each other. My worries about my awful year suddenly evaporated. I'd never been any farther west than Front Royal, Virginia, but I could picture myself climbing rocks in the Superstition Mountains under the desert sun, stopping every now and then to consult the *Life* magazine article. When the blazing sun went down, Gretchen and I would roast hot dogs over a fire while the coyotes howled and the ghost of the old Dutchman roamed the hills, protecting his gold.

Mrs. Sharp came back to see how we liked the story. "I'm glad you enjoyed it," she said. "You know, John Orrin likes treasure stories, too. He asked me if I had any books about buried treasure and then I remembered the article. Why don't you share it with him?"

I stared at Gretchen in dismay. Share our wonderful *private* story with *him*! Why did John Orrin always have to meddle in everything we did?

Mrs. Sharp led John over to our table. "Kobie and Gretchen just finished reading this exciting story," she told him, practically pushing him in my lap in her enthusiasm to foist his company on us. "I'm sure they'll be happy to let you read it. Maybe the three of you can discuss it then. Isn't it nice to have a common interest?"

I spoke up before she left. "But, Mrs.

Sharp, it's *our* story. You saved it for us. You *gave* it to us."

A frown puckered her forehead. "Well, yes, I gave it to you girls first, but I brought it in for everyone to enjoy. You can take it home with you after the others have looked at it, if you like."

What good was an exclusive, saved-especially-for-us treasure story if she was going to let everybody read it? Of all people, Mrs. Sharp knew how much Gretchen and I liked our little secrets. Nobody else would appreciate the story of the Lost Dutchman Mine — the others would probably think it was dumb.

Then John had to open his mouth and make things worse, as usual. "I don't want to read it," he drawled. "I'll go over there and look at books instead."

"John, I thought you said you wanted to read about the lost mine. When I told you about it, you seemed excited."

"Well, obviously he's not," I said.

Mrs. Sharp's ever-present smile melted. "Kobie, I'm surprised at you! It's not like you to be stingy."

Yes, it was, she just didn't know it. This was the new going-on-twelve Kobie Roberts and she was a lot stingier, among other things, than the old Kobie Roberts.

"The library is for every student in Centreville Elementary," she went on crisply. "All the resources in this room are available to anyone who has a need or an interest. Do you understand?"

Gretchen and John nodded, but I tuned her out, thinking instead of the answer to that riddle: Oh, look at the orange marmalade!

"We're finished with the story," Gretchen told Mrs. Sharp, rescuing me. "John can have it."

The librarian left to stamp books, evidently satisfied we were going to behave ourselves.

"She probably hates me now," I said. "Here, take the stupid article." I shoved the papers across the table to John. "I hope you hate it."

"Kobie!" Gretchen cried. "She didn't mean it," she soothed John. "She never means half of what she says."

"Yes, I do. I meant every syllable. Since *you* came over here, you'll have to put up with me."

"I didn't ask to come over here," John corrected.

"Then why *are* you here?" I demanded. "How come every time I turn around, there *you* are, getting me in trouble? Why did you have to come to our school, anyway? Why didn't you just stay where you were?"

"Because my folks moved here," he answered, unruffled. "If you want to know the truth, when we first came, I sort of liked Centreville. But now I don't think I do."

"Then leave," I said, as if he could pack and go that very minute.

"I wish I could."

"That makes two of us."

John remained composed, calm as a boulder in a hurricane. "Where I came from, people are a lot friendlier."

"That's because they're all as dumb as you."

"Kobie — " Gretchen hated bickering. "If you can't say anything nice to John, don't say anything at all."

"She doesn't really rile me." John's lips curved in that tiny condescending smile that drove me insane.

He was like the ghost of the Lost Dutchman Mine; he would never stop haunting me, no matter where I went. I absolutely had to get in the last word or explode.

"I hate you," I said and turned my back to John.

Then I realized there was one other tactic I hadn't tried yet. Cold War. Instead of losing my temper at him, I'd snipe *indirectly* at him. That way I could still get my licks in and John wouldn't be able to complain.

"Do you smell something rotten?" I asked Gretchen, ignoring John as if he weren't sitting next to me.

She knew what I was up to. "No," she said, prickly with disapproval. "I don't smell anything except books and library paste."

"Well, I do. It smells like — like a dead rat. That's it. Mrs. Sharp probably trapped a rat behind the bookcase and it's rotting."

John was absorbed in the article. "Wow! Did you read the part about how much money they think the gold is worth?" he asked Gretchen, roundly ignoring *me*. "Millions and millions of dollars! I'd like to find that mine, wouldn't you?"

Before Gretchen could reply, I said, "Did you hear anything, Gretch? Must be the wind."

John said, "Those clues shouldn't be too hard to figure out. The patches only cover one or two spots, you can see the rest plain as day. I bet we could figure out where that mine is."

"Awfully loud wind," I remarked. "And hot, too." I fanned myself with the riddle book. "Just a lot of hot air."

When library period was finally over, I breezed past Mrs. Sharp's desk without saying good-bye to her the way I usually did.

"Kobie." Her voice reeled me back.

"Yes, Mrs. Sharp?"

"You didn't take the article." It was lying on the table where John had left it. "I thought you wanted to take it home."

"No, thanks." I wasn't about to touch it after John had his grubby paws all over it. "You can let other kids read it," I offered grandly, although my image was already tarnished.

Mrs. Sharp regarded me while my class streamed out behind us. When Gretchen paused at the desk, too, the librarian indicated she'd like to speak to me alone. When I was the last one in the library, she said, "Kobie, lately you seem a little unhappy. Is there anything you'd like to talk about?"

"No."

"I'd like to help, if I can."

"I don't need any help. I'm fine." But I did need help. I felt weird, as if I were plummeting down an endless mine shaft. Nothing was going right and it seemed as if nothing would, ever again.

"Well, if you feel like talking, my door is always open."

My gaze traveled past her ear, outside the window to the gray house on the hill. What would I talk to her about, even if I decided to trust her again? What the little chick said when he found an orange in his mother's nest? Mrs. Sharp would never understand that, besides the falling feeling, I also felt shuttered and closed-in, like the Hammer Man's house.

In fact, finding somebody who *would* understand was as remote as getting the Hammer Man to come out of his house.

Chapter 11

That night in bed I thought of a plan. The ultimate revenge. A plan that would fix John Orrin's wagon permanently and help me regain my position in room 10.

The weird feeling was still hanging over me as I brushed my teeth and changed into my pajamas. I felt sort of lonely, but it was too late to call Gretchen and I didn't want to talk to my parents. It wasn't that kind of loneliness.

Instead I piled my stuffed animals on my bed. All twenty-seven of them, ranging in size from my two-foot-tall panda bear to Ellsworth, a miniature elephant.

I had a system for arranging the stuffed animals and it took me about fifteen minutes to get them in the proper order. The big panda went against the wall, Dixie the mouse was next to him and below him the white rabbit with the music box in its tummy that didn't work anymore, and so on until there was just enough room left for me to crawl under the covers.

It was very cozy with all my old friends crowded around me. Of course I was much too old to sleep with stuffed animals, but I figured it wouldn't hurt to have them there a little while. When I was younger, I used to sleep with my stuffed animals because I was afraid of the dark. But then after I'd fallen asleep, I'd pitch them out one by one so I'd have room to turn over. One time I bonked my head on the white rabbit with the broken music box in its stomach, nearly giving myself a concussion. I transferred the rabbit down to the foot of the bed, where it wouldn't do any damage.

I lay back against my pillow with Ellsworth in the crook of my elbow, watching the headlights from the cars on Lee Highway graze my ceiling. The events of the day tumbled through my head like socks in an automatic dryer. So far John Orrin had evaded me at every junction. I just couldn't win, no matter what I did. It wasn't fair.

What could I do to get back at him?

I heard my mother in the hall, adjusting the thermostat on the wall outside my room. We had a constant battle over the furnace. My room was like a deep freeze all year long except in July and August, when it became a sauna. I tweaked the thermostat dial up to eighty degrees or so every night before I went to bed. Naturally my mother would hear the blower come on and come down the hall to turn it back down.

Sometimes my mother came in my room to kiss me good night again or just look in to see if I was still breathing. Once I was dozing off with my arm dangling over the side of the mattress. She tiptoed into my room and moved my arm, to keep the circulation from being cut off, I guess. It felt good when she did that, like hitting a warm spot while wading in a cold lake. Lately my mother hardly ever checked on me after I went to bed. Maybe she was too tired . . . or maybe she didn't care anymore.

Hearing her now, I flopped over in bed and dangled my arm over the edge of the mattress. When my mother switched the thermostat outside my door, I pretended to be asleep. Through my squinched eyelids, I sensed her inspecting me, but she didn't come in and move my arm. She eased the door shut, until the light from the hallway narrowed to a strip of yellow across my rug, then left.

Well! Obviously my mother didn't care whether her only daughter's arm turned black and dropped off before morning. I tried to convince myself I was too old anyway to be tucked into bed. After all, I was going on twelve. Only babies like Beverly, the twerp who sat with my mother on the bus, slept with stuffed animals and wanted to be kissed good night every two seconds. I flung my animals on the floor, then slumped back against my pillow, fighting tears of anger. Why was I crying? Not over my mother — *she* certainly didn't care. If I died from gangrene of the arm, my mother would probably give all my stuffed animals to Beverly. I think I despised Beverly almost as much as I despised John Orrin.

If only I could get rid of Beverly and John just by hating them to another place, another planet, even, the way I tried to will the Hammer Man to leave his house. I had as much chance of getting rid of John as I did of finding the Lost Dutchman Mine.

And then it hit me. The wonderful, brilliant plan.

Maybe I couldn't send John Orrin to another planet, but I *could* cause him to get suspended, maybe sent away from Centreville forever.

I couldn't wait until morning came so I could get started.

* * *

"A fake treasure map?" Gretchen echoed the next day in the Honeysuckle Hideout. "That's the joke you're going to play on John?"

"We already know he's nuts over buried treasure stories," I said, zipping my jacket up to my neck. It was pretty chilly in the hideout. Our days of outdoor recess were numbered, which meant I had to hurry and put my plan into motion. "I draw this fake treasure map and plant it in his desk. He finds it." I slackened my jaw, miming John discovering the map.

"Then what?" Gretchen prompted.

I resumed my normal expression. "He starts following the clues. First he has to go over to the baseball diamond, then he has to go over to the monkey bars, and then the swings — "

"Wait a minute," she interrupted. "You mean the map will be this playground? Kobie, why would anyone believe there's a treasure buried on the playground?"

"Let me finish. He goes back up to the blacktop, then around to the water fountain. He goes all over the place and gets confused. Then the map leads him back down the hill and over to the old fence we found, until he winds up — " I paused triumphantly, having reached the best part. "At the Dairy Queen!"

"The Dairy Queen?" Gretchen still didn't catch on. "The treasure's going to be buried at the Dairy Queen?"

"There is no treasure! The whole idea is to get him *over there* so we can tell Mrs. Harmon! That's the joke!" Of course my plan was more than a joke. The principal was sure to suspend John for sneaking over to the Dairy Queen, the one rule he couldn't stand to have disobeyed. "Won't it be a riot? And it's sure to work!"

"I hate to tell you this," Gretchen said, "but your idea is full of holes."

"What holes? I've thought of every angle. I can't lose on this one."

"Kobic, what makes you so sure that John will fall for a phony treasure map? He wasn't born yesterday, you know. He gets pretty good grades, better than mine. Better than *yours*." She *would* have to bring up my miserable report card.

"Have you forgotten who the best artist in the school is? I can draw a map that would fool anyone. My map will make him believe there's a buried treasure out here somewhere. It can't fail."

She jammed her hands into the pockets of her coat. "I don't like the idea of getting John in trouble."

"What trouble? It's a *joke*, Gretch. Jokes

are supposed to be funny. Why aren't you laughing?"

She looked at me, her blue eyes serious. "Because this one isn't funny. I know you, Kobie Roberts. I know how your devious pea brain works. Mr. Magyn suspends kids who are caught at the Dairy Queen. That's what you want, isn't it? To get him suspended."

"So what if I do? He's always getting me in trouble, why can't I try to get him back once? You won't say anything, will you? You're still my best friend," I added, as if that prevented her from telling on me.

Gretchen was quiet. I suddenly sensed our friendship straining at the seams. Would I lose her, my one and only friend, over my need for revenge?

"I won't tell," she promised, "but don't expect me to help, either."

She really believed in sticking to her principles. So did I, though I wasn't sure what they were. I only knew that I had to go through with this.

I started my map as soon as I got home from school. In order for the map to be credible, it had to look old-timey, kind of brown and ragged around the edges. A wrinkled grocery sack ripped into a rough rectangle looked fairly authentic by the time I was done "aging" it. Sepia crayon gave the map a faded, hundred-years-ago appearance, like the brown inks people used in the olden days.

"Kobie! What are you doing?" my mother shouted from the kitchen. "Have you swept the basement yet?"

"I'm busy," I called back.

"Doing what, your homework?"

"No," I answered truthfully. "I'm working on a project."

As if transported by magic, my mother materialized at my door, still wearing her cafeteria uniform. "I asked you an hour ago to sweep the basement. The man is coming tomorrow morning to fix the hot water tank and the basement is a hog pen."

"Basements are supposed to be dirty," I said, not looking up from my map. "He won't mind. In fact, he'd probably be more suspicious if it was clean. You know, wonder what we really do in our basement to keep it so clean. Instead of fixing the hot water heater, he'd spend all his time hunting for a printing press, thinking we're counterfeiters or something — "

"Stop changing the subject. Why haven't you done it?"

"I told you, I'm busy." Carefully I drew a north-west-south-east compass in one corner of my map. If I messed up, it would be her fault, yammering at me.

"If you're not doing your homework, then you're not too busy to do what I asked you," she said. "Every time I want you to do something, I have to whoop and holler to get you to do it. I'm tired of telling you things over and over, Kobie. In this house, we all have to do our share."

Her complaints were the same ones I've heard for years. I almost wished my mother would dredge up a new set of gripes. "I'll sweep the basement in a little while," I told her.

"No, you won't. You'll drag out whatever it is you're doing until tonight or the next day so you conveniently won't have to work. You won't turn your hand to do a thing around here anymore. My mother told me girls your age got lazy and she was right."

"If you knew I was going to get lazy, why do you try to make me work?" I was swimming in deep water, but it was too late to take the words back.

"If your father heard how you sass me . . . but no, you're nice when he's around."

"That's because he's nice to *me*. He tells me stories and makes me things. He doesn't scream at me night and day to clean the house."

Her eyes got moist as she chewed her bottom lip. I had hurt her feelings, but it was the truth. My father *was* nicer. "I hate this stage you're going through," she said. "I wish you were a cute little first grader again, like Beverly."

I had that coming but it still rankled, being compared to that little twit. "Then get Beverly to sweep your old basement," I snapped. "Since you're so crazy about her."

"Are you jealous of that little girl? Kobie, you should be ashamed."

"Well, you sit with her every single day on the bus."

"Where am I supposed to sit? On the hood?" she countered. "You don't want me sitting with you, you've made it quite clear."

I didn't know what I wanted anymore, except for this conversation to end. "All right! I'll sweep the basement, even though I think it's dumb to put on airs for the hot water tank man."

"We don't put on airs!" she retorted. "The place is filthy. When you used to swing down in the basement, you swept it every week. Now you don't go down there anymore, so you couldn't care less if the dirt piles up to the ceiling. You only do something when it suits your purpose."

"I *said* I'd do it, didn't I?"

"I'll do it myself," my mother said curtly. "Asking you to help a little around here is like asking a stick." She flounced into her room to change out of her uniform.

Through the heat register in my room, I could hear my mother down in the basement, sweeping the floor with resentful strokes of the push broom. I felt a twinge of guilt. If only she hadn't asked me to do a chore when I was working on my fake treasure map. But the map was more important to me than impressing some guy coming to fix our hot water tank.

I had to put the map aside to eat supper. As we ate beans and franks, I expected my mother, who came to the table with dust in her hair, to blab to my father. She never said a word about our argument.

After supper, my father went into the living room to watch the news. I lay on the rug beside him with my arithmetic book (merely a front) and my map. Usually my mother watched television with us, but tonight she attacked the dishes immediately after supper.

I decorated the margins of my map with dragons and sea monsters, like the old maps back when people thought there were only boundless oceans and strange creatures beyond their land.

"That looks like something I've seen before," my father said, glancing over my shoulder.

"What?"

"Those monsters you're drawing. Remind me of . . . I don't know." He scratched his head. "Oh, yeah, that paper I got when I crossed the equator."

I held my breath. Did he also remember where it was? "Dad, you told me I could have that paper but we can't find it. Do you remember where you put it?"

"Oh, it's around here someplace." He clicked off the TV and went back out to the kitchen.

I stared at the picture tube as the square of light diminished until it vanished altogether. If only I had the King Neptune paper, my troubles would be over. I would have a map of my own to guide me. Then going on twelve wouldn't be so murky and mysterious.

Planting the fake treasure map in John Orrin's desk turned out to be the simplest part of the entire scheme. John took a pirate book out of the library and brought it to school every day to read during free period. The library book was left conspicuously on top of his textbooks stacked in the compartment under his desk. I could see it from where I sat, two seats back.

Because it rained the whole week, Mrs. Harmon kept us indoors during recess. On the second day of indoor recess, we played a boisterous game of musical desks to this hilarious record. I positioned myself so that when Mrs. Harmon lifted the needle of the record player, I was sitting in John's desk. When the song started again, I slipped the folded treasure map in the back of his library book. Easy as pie.

Now all I had to do was wait. Wait for John to discover the map in his book. Wait for the rain to stop so we could have recess outside. Wait for the stupid country fly to blunder into the crafty spider's web.

Chapter 12

Alert as a bird dog, I watched John Orrin every day during free period. He would open his pirate book and read, slowly and methodically, following along with his finger. John made good grades, as Gretchen said, but he wasn't what you'd call a genius. He studied fiercely, memorizing lists of history dates and spelling words. He read the same way, so it took him forever to get through that stupid library book.

And then he found it. One morning he turned the page and my map drifted out. I held my breath as he unfolded it. Did it *really* look like a map or just a grocery bag with brown crayoned marks on it? If John immersed himself in stories the way I did, he'd be *ready* to believe it was a treasure map. After he'd been reading about pirates and buried treasure for a week, his head should have been brimming with visions of gold dubloons and Jolly Roger flags.

I couldn't see his face as he examined my map, but he stuck it in his shirt pocket and patted the flimsy material, as if guarding a secret.

"He fell for it," I whispered to Gretchen.

We had outdoor recess that day for the first time since the rain let up. It was sunny, but a stiff breeze chased leaves ahead of us as Gretchen and I loped down the mud-slicked hill to the Honeysuckle Hideout. Inside the tunnel, I crouched on the sodden floor so I could spy on John.

"He's by the basketball net, right on schedule," I reported gleefully. "He's checking the map. Now he's counting off the paces. In thirty-three steps he should be behind the baseball diamond. Take bigger steps, dummy! He won't reach the baseball diamond in a hundred steps, the dumb way he walks."

Gretchen refused to watch John bumble around the playground with my phony treasure map. "I still think it's mean," she commented in a low voice.

"What's mean?" I said. "He's having a great time out there, Gretch. Nobody ever invites him to play. For the first time since he came here, he's actually got something to do during recess."

"You know what I'm talking about. When he winds up at the Dairy Queen."

I clucked my tongue. "Into each life a little rain must fall," I said, quoting my father again.

She stared at the old man's house on the hill, defiantly ignoring my running commentary of John's progress.

Her objection didn't bother me much. As long as she was with me in the hideout, I knew she was still my friend. I resumed spying. John was spinning like a windmill on the blacktop, evidently trying to determine which way was north-by-northeast. I had deliberately made the directions tricky — if the map was too easy, he'd never buy it.

"Not that way," I coaxed. "Over *there*. At the rate he's going, he won't get to the Dairy Queen before next year. He can't even find the next clue, which is the water fountain. It's as plain as the nose on your face but he's too dumb — "

"Kobie, it's him! He's coming out! The Hammer Man!" Gretchen yanked me around.

The gray house above our hideout was blank-shuttered and unearthly silent, as usual. But the old man was indeed sauntering down the hill toward his shed. He wore a leather jacket and no hat — the wind tousled his long white hair. He didn't seem to be armed with a hammer or any other lethal weapon, but looks could be deceiving.

At last, the chance we'd been waiting for! With Gretchen distracting the Hammer Man, I could sneak in his shed and collect the necessary evidence. Then we'd go to the police and nail the Hammer Man. I grinned at my own pun. In one wonderful dazzling day, I would get rid of John Orrin and expose the Hammer Man! People would call me Famous Girl Sleuth like Nancy Drew, or maybe simply the Heroine of Centreville.

"We have to hurry," I said, pushing Gretchen toward the entrance. "He might not stay in his shed very long."

Gretchen balked halfway through the tunnel. "We're not going up there?"

"Yes! What do you think? We've talked about our plan a hundred times."

"Kobie, I don't want to do this."

"We *have* to," I screeched. "It's our last chance to be famous! We probably won't see the old man again till next spring."

Still she wouldn't budge. "If Mrs. Harmon sees us off school property, we'll be suspended just like John."

"Honestly, Gretch, do you want to be a nobody the rest of your life? Do you think a real hero like Admiral Byrd worried about leaving school property when he flew over the South Pole?" Then I remembered the reward money. "This time tomorrow," I said enticingly, "you could be in Woolworth's on the biggest shopping spree in the world. Don't forget the reward money."

"I don't want the money," she said and I realized she was nearly in tears. "I'm scared. I'm afraid to go up there."

In my exuberance to make a name for myself, I had overlooked the danger of our mission. "I'm scared, too," I admitted. "But we'll be together and it'll be over before you know it. Think of Admiral Byrd."

"He was in an airplane," she said, wiping her eyes and smiling. "We'll be on the ground."

"Then you'll do it?" Without Gretchen, I couldn't catch a gnat, much less a criminal.

She released a shuddering breath. "I'll do it. Let's go before I chicken out again." She parted the curtain of honeysuckle that concealed the entrance to our hideout.

Outside, I saw Mrs. Harmon gabbing with Mrs. Wright up on the blacktop. A few kids swung from the monkey bars, but they didn't notice us as we scuttled to the boundary of dense undergrowth that divided school property from the old man's property.

Heads down, we ran through rain-soaked weeds, wet horsetail, and snarly goose grass that tripped us about every other step. Briars snagged our socks and soon our legs were crisscrossed with whip-thin scratches.

Up on the hill, I glanced behind us again. The teachers were still talking. Bright figures of our classmates skipped around the blacktop, like scraps of colored construction paper. For an instant I longed to be with them, joining in their silly, ordinary games.

Then it dawned on me that what Gretchen and I were doing was *real*. Away from the safety of the hideout, we weren't idly speculating whether the man who lived in the gray house was a murderer, but were actually carrying out one of my schemes.

Thousands of acorns from the ancient oak trees, like marbles spilled from a giant bucket, made sneaking up on the Hammer Man even more treacherous. We slipped and slid, clutching each other to keep from falling, until we got the giggles.

"Shhh!" I cautioned as we approached the shed. The building was bigger than it appeared from the hideout. The warped boards hadn't seen a coat of paint this century.

Gretchen hung back, her eyes round and frightened.

"It'll be okay. Come on." I sounded braver than I felt. What if the Hammer Man had seen us? He might be sitting behind that door with his trusty hammer lying across his knees, just waiting. . . .

Gretchen nudged me, pointing to a knothole in the side of the shed.

"Good idea," I whispered. "Let's see if he's in there."

Before I could peek through the hole, Gretchen drew me back again. Her hand was over her mouth, muffling a laugh. Was she hysterical with fear?

"Kobie, suppose this isn't a shed at all, but an *outhouse* and he's in there — " Her pent-up laughter escaped in a spluttery outburst.

Laugh attacks were nothing new to us. They struck any time, any place, like a tornado. Last week in assembly when the second graders were doing the Hokey-Pokey, Gretchen and I had a giggle-fit. Mrs. Harmon separated us, but even then we couldn't quit. After Gretchen was moved four rows away from me in the auditorium, all I had to do was stick my left leg out in the aisle and shake it like the little kids were doing on stage, and Gretchen doubled up.

It was the same thing now. We collapsed in a heap in the acorn-studded grass, rolling on the acorns and laughing so hard a whole herd of criminals could have stampeded us.

The door to the outbuilding squeaked inward. The old man sat just inside the door, not on a toilet seat as we had pictured, but on a tool bench, surrounded by tools hanging from nails: saws and pliers and *hammers*. My plan suddenly winged out the window. The Hammer Man had caught us instead.

He wasn't at all the hardened criminal I expected to see. White feathery hair fringed a high forehead. His skin was the texture of leather, like his jacket. Behind rimless glasses, clear blue eyes appraised us.

He spoke first. "Well, hello there." His voice was creaky, like the chains of my basement swing, but friendly. "I know you two. You're the girls always hidin' in the brambles."

"You've seen us?" I asked, incredulous. After months of spying on his house, I was shocked to learn he'd been spying on *us* at the same time!

"Sure, I've seen you. I'm not blind." He

cocked his head at me. "You're the big-mouthed one, always yellin' at that little blond-haired fella."

My face reddened. The Hammer Man had heard me teasing John Orrin!

Gretchen grinned. "That's Kobie, all right. My name is Gretchen Farris. The big mouth is Kobie Roberts."

"I'm Thomas Robey. Pleased to meet you." He extended his hand. Gretchen shook it politely. "What're you girls doing up here? Payin' a social visit?" he asked.

"We were just —" Gretchen looked at me.

"Well, we were —" My voice died away. I couldn't very well tell him what we were *really* doing. "We were — hunting for buried treasure!"

Mr. Robey chuckled. "Buried treasure, huh? You won't find none on this place. I've been here eighty-four years and I ain't seen no treasure yet!"

"You've been here that long?" I marvelled.

"All my life. I was born here. 'Spect I'll die here."

It was obvious Mr. Robey wasn't the Hammer Man. Up close, he resembled some-body's nice old grandfather more than a murderer. Deep in my heart, I knew I had used the legend of the Hammer Man to create a new secret project. In order to convince Gretchen, I began believing my own story. Even deeper down inside, I think Gretchen knew I was making it up but went along with me because we were friends.

"What d'you girls do down in the bushes?" Mr. Robey demanded. "I see you down there pert' near every day."

Gretchen replied, "Oh, we read, mostly Nancy Drew mysteries, and sometimes Kobie draws pictures. She tells really neat stories, too."

"Is that so?" Mr. Robey focused his attention on me. "How come you don't play with the other children yonder? I never see you jumpin' rope or playin' ball. Why is that?"

"Those kids are morons," I said scornfully. "Gretchen and I have more fun by ourselves."

"It's nice you've got a good friend." Mr. Robey gazed at the activity on the blacktop. "My son and daughter-in-law live with me," he rambled. "The woman means well, but she's always fussin' over me." His voice cracked as he mimicked his daughter-in-law. " 'Don't sit in a draft, Dad. Put this rug over your legs.' Like I said, she means well. Ever' chance I get, I run out here and hide, like you all do in your bushes, just to have a minute's peace. But when she's babysittin' me, I park myself in a big easy chair by the parlor window and watch the children on the playground."

I couldn't imagine a more boring way to kill time. And I thought I had it bad, stuck in dull old Willow Springs.

"That little fella out there reminds me of when I was his age." A solitary figure stood by the empty monkey bars. John Orrin! "I was all by my lonesome, just like he is, day after day. Seems like nobody wants him around. Nobody liked me, neither, so I know just how he feels."

Mr. Robey's clear blue eyes were disarming, as if he could see right through me. I felt his remarks were mainly for my benefit. I didn't want to talk about John and how lonely he was.

I blurted out the first thing that flitted into my head. "You ought to come out west with us. Gretchen and I are going to Arizona someday." Her expression said this was news to her. "Out to the Superstition Mountains to find the Lost Dutchman Mine. It's loaded with gold. There'll be plenty for the three of us."

Mr. Robey chuckled again. "Go out west and find a gold mine! Glory be! My daughter-in-law won't let me out of her sight, much less let me go traipsin' off to Arizona."

"She would if you tell her about all the gold you'll bring back. It's hidden in the mountains, but we've got a map — " I broke off, suddenly remembering the trap I had set for John. He was still following the phony treasure map and only had one more clue to unravel before he'd be off school property.

Mr. Robey nodded, as if he were actually considering our expedition. "The riches of the world are often buried," he allowed. "Gold, diamonds. Gold is usually covered by ugly rock and you don't even know it's there. Diamonds don't show their fire till they're cut. Kind of like people."

"Like people?" Gretchen asked. "How?"

"Well sir, you have to take the time to dig beneath the surface on some people. Outside, they might look like a humble rock. But way down deep, they could be bright and shiny like a diamond, or gold. You have to look mighty hard." His sharp scrutiny was making me uncomfortable, as if he were judging me.

Down the hill, John measured off paces, skirting our hideout.

"We should go," Gretchen said to me. "Mrs. Harmon will probably blow her whistle any minute for us to line up on the blacktop." I suspected she planned to detour John away from the Dairy Queen so he wouldn't get in trouble. I didn't really care — the joke had gone far enough.

"You'd better skedaddle then," Mr. Robey agreed. "I like your company, but maybe you ought to come back another time, when you're not supposed to be in school. When I sold the land for your school, it was on the condition that no children would wander over the line on my property."

"Why?" I asked, sidetracked by curiosity. "What difference does it make if we play in the bushes at the bottom of the hill? We don't hurt anything."

"It's not my property I'm worried about. It's the children. There's an abandoned well somewhere in the brush down there. At one time I had it fenced off, but the fence keeled over. My son was going to locate the blamed thing and cover it proper, but the kids have been good at staying off my property." Until now, he implied.

"We know where it is! We could show your son so he could — " I stopped horrified.

John Orrin, intently following the final instruction on my map, was heading right for the well! Even if he stubbed his foot against one of the square rocks that bordered the rim of the well, he might not be able to catch himself in time.

"Kobie!" Gretchen cried. "The well — !"

I barreled down the hill, screaming at the top of my lungs. "John! Don't take another step! John — stop!"

He looked up from his counting, startled. Then his foot vaulted through the vines camouflaging the opening of the well and he crashed through the brambly net.

Chapter 13

I reached the well first, careful not to stumble over the slablike wall. My heart was thumping like crazy. If John was killed or hurt, it was all my fault! I never meant to hurt him, only have him suspended. And even that was terrible, now that I thought about it.

Slithering across the ledge on my stomach, I leaned over the yawning hole. My fear of heights came roaring back, forcing me to withdraw before I could look down. How deep was the well? And how could I help John get out? Even with a ladder, it was doubtful I'd have enough nerve to climb down there.

I cupped my hands in a megaphone. "John! Are you okay?"

"Kobie?" His voice didn't sound that far down. "Is that you? Yeah, I'm okay. Help me up, will you?"

He was asking me to help him! *Me!* After all I had done to him, humiliated him, called him names, plotted and planned and schemed to get rid of him. And still he wanted my help.

Gathering what little courage I could muster, I crawled out over the rock and looked down into the well. John Orrin's face tilted upward. To my everlasting relief, the well wasn't very deep at all! He teetered on a pile of debris, leaves and rocks and stuff that had either fallen or been dumped into the dried-up well, the top of his head only a few inches from the mossy rim. He really was okay!

I stretched my arm down into the pit, gripping the square stone with my other hand. He grabbed my arm with both hands, clinging tightly. When I pulled, he managed to gain a foothold on a rock protruding from the side of the well. By this time Gretchen had arrived. The two of us tugged on his belt and hauled him over the side.

Panting, he rested against the stone wall. "That was something! Like to scared me to death!"

"You aren't hurt, are you?" Gretchen asked anxiously.

"Naw. I bumped my knee going down but that's it."

"Let's see." He had no choice but to roll

up his pants leg. Above the frayed hem of his sock, a purplish knot was forming. "You'd better go to the nurse. It might be sprained. What do you think, Kobie?"

What did *I* think? That was like asking Dracula if he thought a mosquito bite should be treated. It was my fault John fell in the well in the first place. Me and my stupid treasure map.

Kathy Stall and Marcia Dittier tore through the brambles to drag us back on school property. From there, we went straight to the office.

Mr. Magyn was not nearly as lenient as he'd been the last time. He wrote notes for Gretchen and John to take to their parents before excusing John to the nurse's office and letting Gretchen return to class. But instead of writing a note for my parents, he had my mother paged over the PA system.

She must have raced upstairs because she got there in about four seconds flat. Her face was drained, as if she were afraid something awful had happened to me. When she saw me slouched in Mr. Magyn's office, obviously all right, she looked so relieved that I felt worse than ever.

"Kobie was caught off school property during recess," Mr. Magyn informed her. "Along with Gretchen Farris and John

Orrin. The Orrin boy fell into an unused well on Mr. Robey's property. Fortunately he was not hurt seriously, but he could have been. Because this is a first offense for these children, at least to my knowledge, I'm leaving disciplinary action up to their parents. But the next time — " He left his threat unfinished, letting my vivid imagination fill in a suitably horrid punishment.

I could tell my mother was infuriated by the incident. All she said after the principal dismissed us was a terse, "I'll deal with you later."

It was strange going back to class. Everybody in room 10 knew John and Gretchen and I were in trouble, but Mrs. Harmon continued the arithmetic lesson as if nothing had happened. Mrs. Harmon never made a big deal after a kid came back from the office, like some teachers did. I slipped into my seat and got out my arithmetic book. Kathy Stall tapped the corner of her own textbook, so I could find the right page. Usually she ignored me totally or made some remark to Marcia Dittier. I guess she felt sorry for me.

The door opened again and John Orrin limped to his seat.

"Are you all right, John?" Mrs. Harmon inquired.

"Yes, ma'am," he replied. He threw me

that funny little smile. Apparently his leg wasn't sprained.

But my friendship with Gretchen was definitely wounded. Because of my obsession to get revenge, she was in as much trouble as I was.

At lunchtime, Gretchen hurried ahead of me to get into the serving line. I plopped down at our table and emptied the contents of my lunch bag. If Gretchen wanted to eat with Kathy and Marcia from now on, I could hardly blame her. When she marched over to our table with John Orrin limping behind her, I was so stunned I dropped my finger sandwich on the floor.

"Kobie, you're such a slob," Gretchen chided, breaking her butter cookie in two and handing me half. "Here. So you won't starve."

"Boy, I was scared. I thought Mr. Magyn was going to suspend us," John said, pulling up a chair. "Didn't you?"

I stared at Gretchen, but she merely shrugged. Why was John sitting at our table? Didn't he realize my purpose all along was to have him expelled? Surely he must have known the map was a fake. He probably even knew that I had drawn it and stuck it in his library book. I still couldn't understand why he wanted to eat lunch with me.

Gretchen said, "Did you notice how sloppy Mr. Magyn's desk was? And he's always telling us in assembly how important it is to be neat and organized!"

"He couldn't even find his own telephone!" John laughed. You would never have thought that only an hour ago John was at the bottom of an abandoned well.

In a rare display of generosity, I gave my half of the butter cookie to him.

"That's your favorite," Gretchen said, surprised.

"I'm not hungry." I wasn't. Unrelated thoughts whirled around my brain. The Hammer Man, the fake map, the terror of watching John fall into the well. Events that I had caused. Recalling what Mr. Robey had said about looking beneath the surface for the true value in other people, I wondered what other people saw in me. Gold and diamonds . . . or brass and rhinestones.

My mother didn't speak as we walked up our steep driveway. I still felt terrible. The sky was November-gray, reflecting my mood. There was no point stepping on the Moonstone for luck. Wishing couldn't change what I had done. Much as I longed to retreat into my tree house, I had to face the music.

"Go to your room," my mother said, unlocking the door. "I'll be there in a minute."

I threw myself across my bed, clutched my stuffed panda to my chest, and began to sob. I *hated* to cry. Crying was for little kids, not somebody going on twelve. But it seemed like the closer I got to my twelfth birthday, the more I cried.

The mattress dented under my mother's weight as she sat next to me. "What's wrong, Kobie?"

"I'm miserable!" I was crying so hard, the word came out *mi-huh-is-huh-ra-huh-ble*. "Nobody knows!"

"I think I do," she said. "I was almost twelve myself, once."

"Are you going to tell Dad what I did today?"

"Shouldn't I? He has a right to know."

"Then he'll be mad at me, too!" I sobbed harder than ever.

"I expect so. Sit up, Kobie. I want to talk to you."

I obeyed, snuffling. She brushed my damp bangs out of my eyes. Her touch felt comforting, like the time she moved my arm when it was hanging over the side of the bed.

"You can't go on only showing your good side to your father," she said. "He knows you're not perfect, Kobie."

"But I don't want him mad at me."

"And I can be?"

I plucked at a tuft of chenille on my ratty old bedspread. "You know what I mean."

"You mean you like your father better than me." She stated this matter-of-factly, yet I knew her feelings were hurt. I didn't want to hurt anyone, but I seemed to be hurting people right and left lately.

"I don't like him *better*." I chose my words carefully. "It's just that he tells me stories and he makes me things. He doesn't yell at me all the time like you do."

"That's because he doesn't see your room like the wreck of the Hesperus, the way I do. And he doesn't know you'd only wash your hair once a year unless I got on you about it. Your father leaves for work early and he doesn't get home until suppertime. It's my job to see to it you get to school looking halfway decent and you do your homework. It's tough being a mother."

"It's no picnic being a kid, either."

"I know. Remember all those things my mother told me about girls growing up? How they get lazy and how they sass their mothers?"

I nodded. She could publish a book of my grandmother's corny sayings.

"Who do you think told my mother about raising girls? *Her* mother — your great-grandmother. And what my grandmother said still holds true. Because even though times change, people don't. Girls — and boys, too — go through the same stages. Growing up is no picnic, as you put it."

A pattern was beginning to emerge in my mind. "You were just like me when you were twelve, weren't you?"

"Exactly. That's why I can't come down on you too hard." My father had mentioned that my mother and I were alike in ways I wouldn't understand until I was older. Well, I was older now. And I was starting to understand.

"Remind me to tell you about the time I chopped the fur collar off Nancy Marsteller's coat because I was jealous." She laughed at the recollection.

I hadn't heard that story but I knew Nancy Marsteller was the doctor's daughter, the rich girl in town, and that my mother once snipped off Nancy's eyelashes with manicure scissors. Evidently my mother couldn't be trusted with sharp objects. But she had *picked on* Nancy Marsteller — did even worse things than I did to John. At least his clothes and eyelashes were intact. I wasn't proud of what I had done to him. Part of the reason I was feeling so guilty was that John never tried to fight back. Nancy Marsteller probably got her revenge when my mother had to go to Dr. Marsteller's for a shot, by making her father bring out his blunt needle. But John always took whatever I dished out. Maybe Gretchen was right again — maybe we *could* have a third person in our group at lunchtime.

"Were you and Nancy ever friends?" I asked.

"Yes. I thought she was stuck-up because she was rich, but when I got to know her, Nancy became one of my closest friends."

My mother had loads of friends back in the old days. Not one exclusive friend, but all kinds, both girls and boys. That was probably the key to being popular.

Then I remembered other stories my mother had told me, about her and her sister Lil when they were growing up in Manassas. I remembered all the things my mother had made me, too, like the pie-dough roll-ups she always fixed whenever she baked a pie and the skirts and blouses she sewed for me. My father wasn't any nicer than my mother, I realized — they were simply different people.

It was her turn to ask a question. "Think you can stand having me work in your school the rest of the year?"

So that had been a sore spot with her, too. I had to be honest. "Well . . . it sort of cramps my style."

"It cramps my style to have a daughter who won't sit with me on the bus or go through my serving line. Actually, it hurts," she said, equally sincere.

Tears welled up in my eyes again. "Mom — "

"It's okay," she said. "I didn't want to be seen with my mother either when I was your age. You could buy lunch once in a while, though, for old time's sake."

"I'm sorry I'm such a brat," I said, hoping she got my real message.

"So am I." She hugged me. "I'm afraid it's too late to send you back."

I snuggled in her arms for a moment.

"Sit still," she ordered. "I've got a couple of things for you." She came back a few moments later, with a yellowed paper and what looked like a packet of seeds. She gave me the paper first. "I found this the other day when I was rooting through the cedar chest."

The paper was fragile and worn along the creases, a certificate with some Latin jibberish lettered across the top. An anchor was stenciled over the words in the center and linked chains formed a nautical border.

" 'Domain of Neptunus Rex,' " I read

haltingly. "What's that mean?" My parents were forever bragging about taking Latin in school.

"The domain of King Neptune," she translated.

"The Neptune paper!" I yelled. "You found it!" The paper was strange, declaring to all "Mermaids, Whales, Sea Serpents, Porpoises, Sharks, Dolphins, Eels, Skates, Crabs, Lobsters and other Living Things of the Sea that on this day in Latitude 0000 and Longitude 175 degrees West there appeared within Our Royal Domain the U.S.S. *Griffin* bound South for the Equator."

I read the rest of the paper out loud. " 'That the said Vessel and Officers and Crew thereof have been inspected and passed by Us and Our Royal Staff and that Samuel Howard Roberts' — that's Dad! — 'having been found worthy to be numbered as one of Us has been initiated into the Solemn Mysteries of the Ancient Order of the Deep.' " Two signatures were scrawled in the lower left corner, Neptunus Rex, Ruler of the Raging Main, and Davy Jones, His Majesty's Scribe.

My father's Neptune paper. I gulped down a big lump of disappointment. It didn't explain anything about what it was *like* to cross the equator. None of the

"Solemn Mysteries of the Deep" were spelled out. I placed the paper on my bedside table. It was mine to keep, but I was still on my own, without any map or magic document to guide me.

"What's the other thing?" I asked my mother, feeling gloomy again.

She laid a packet of marigold seeds in my lap. The color photograph on the front was faded, the once-bright marigolds a pale, ghostly yellow. Tiny seeds rattled inside; the packet had never been unsealed.

"I'm going to tell you a story," she announced. "One you've never heard."

I settled back against my panda, holding the seed package loosely between two fingers.

"Not too long ago, or so it seems to me, somebody knocked on the door. It took me a while to answer it, because I was expecting you and I couldn't move too fast." So this happened before I was born. My mother went on, "A woman stood on the porch. She had blonde hair and spoke with an accent."

"Who was she?" I asked, mystified.

"A real estate agent, trying to drum up business, I guess. She handed me her business card and this packet of seeds and told me if we ever decided to sell our house, to call her. I was a little annoyed at having to get up for a salesperson, but then I looked at the card and a problem I'd been wrestling with was suddenly solved."

"What problem?"

"Your name." She laughed at the look on my face. "You see, I was positive the baby was going to be a girl so I was only considering girls' names. I had just about decided to call you Pamela before the real estate woman came to the door."

"Pamela! Ugh!" Pamela sounded like a snobby kid who wore lace dresses and ribbons in her hair. It wouldn't have suited me at all. I wasn't a bit like a Pamela.

"Well, it wasn't so bad then," my mother said. "And your father liked it. But when I saw the name on the card, I knew Pamela was all wrong. The woman's name was Kobie something. She was from Germany. I asked about her name and she said it wasn't a nickname. I liked the way the name looked on the card. So when you were born a month later, we named you Kobie. I knew that was a name people would remember."

"I'm glad she didn't hand you the seeds first or I would have been named Marigold," I said wryly. "What happened to the business card?"

"Oh, it got lost in the shuffle of having a baby. But I kept the seeds for you to have one day, a memento of how you got your name."

The story of how I got my name pleased me. I jiggled the seeds in the paper packet. Kobie Roberts. That was my name. A name people would remember. Not Best Artist or Girl Sleuth or Heroine of Centreville. Kobie Roberts was the name I carved in the soft wood of my desk in room 10. It was a name I would take with me as I charted my uncertain course through life. Going on twelve, going on thirteen, going on fourteen . . . no matter how old I was or who my friends were, I would always be Kobie Roberts.

And for now, that was enough.

About the Author

CANDICE F. RANSOM is the author of *Thirteen, Fourteen and Holding,* and *Fifteen at Last,* all involving the further adventures of Kobie Roberts and her best friend Gretchen. She has written thirteen books for Scholastic. Her fourteenth book, *My Sister, the Meanie,* will be published as a Scholastic Hardcover. Ms. Ransom lives in Centreville, Virginia, with her husband and her black cat.

point®

Other books you will enjoy, about real kids like you!